WAKING BEAUTY

WAKING BEAUTY

Brittlyn Gallacher Doyle

SWEETWATER
BOOKS

An Imprint of Cedar Fort, Inc.
Springville, Utah

ISBN 13: 978-1-4621-2053-6

Published by Sweetwater Books, an imprint of Cedar Fort, Inc.
2373 W. 700 S., Springville, UT 84663
Distributed by Cedar Fort, Inc., www.cedarfort.com

LIBRARY OF CONGRESS CATALOGING-IN-PUBLICATION DATA

Names: Doyle, Brittlyn Gallacher, 1987- author.
Title: Waking beauty / Brittlyn Gallacher Doyle.
Description: Springville, Utah : Sweetwater Books, an imprint of Cedar Fort, Inc., [2017] | Summary: "After waking up from her one hundred year sleep, Princess Aurora (who goes by her middle name Claire) is delighted to find everyone in the castle has woken up as well. After getting engaged to the prince who woke her up, she believes everything is perfect until one by one everyone keeps falling back to sleep, and not waking up. Knowing that something with the spell is wrong, Claire, her Prince, and Jamen his knight go on a quest to find the fairy who cast the spell in the first place"-- Provided by publisher.
Identifiers: LCCN 2017017877 (print) | LCCN 2017026709 (ebook) | ISBN 9781462128082 (epub and Moby) | ISBN 9781462120536 (perfect bound : alk. paper)
Subjects: | CYAC: Fairy tales. | LCGFT: Novels. | Adaptations. | Fairy tales. | Fantasy fiction.
Classification: LCC PZ8.D7692 (ebook) | LCC PZ8.D7692 Wak 2017 (print) | DDC [Fic]--dc23
LC record available at https://lccn.loc.gov/2017017877

Cover design by Priscilla Chaves
Cover design © 2017 by Cedar Fort, Inc.
Edited and typeset by Hali Bird and Jessica Romrell

Printed in the United States of America

10 9 8 7 6 5 4 3 2 1

Printed on acid-free paper

For Brandon,
because you knew I could and didn't let me forget it.
But also, and maybe mostly, because you took
that one semester of violin in college.

PROLOGUE

The glittering point of the needle winked at me. I had never seen a spinning wheel, but what else could it be? My hand reached out of its own accord as my feet brought me closer. My breathing quickened and I flinched when I saw the old woman's hunched and haggard form. Somehow, I knew this was Zora. She beckoned with a gnarled finger. I continued moving forward. Slowly. One foot in front of the other. I didn't want to look her in the eye as I arrived at the spindle. My breaths came in quick, little gasps now. I had known this day would come. I was ready. But wait, suddenly I wasn't sure. The needle looked sharp. How would it feel to sleep that long? I didn't even get a chance to say goodbye. I tried to pull my hand back. It wouldn't obey my mental commands and continued toward the needle's point despite my best efforts. Strength was not one of my fairy gifts. Fighting harder to resist the irresistible pull, a faint sheen of perspiration broke out over my forehead as I struggled. I couldn't make any headway. My hand flinched and jerked as I pulled. After a final desperate yank, my strength felt spent and my hand lurched back toward the needle. I glanced over at Zora. She smiled cruelly. I swallowed and opened my mouth to protest when I felt a small sting in my right pointer finger.

"No!" I cried as my eyes flew back to the needle where I saw my finger resting at the very tip. I pulled it back, my mobility restored.

1

I saw a drop of blood, my blood, as it trickled down my hand. A bright flash of light startled me and I turned to find the old woman transformed into something else. She was now young, tall, clothed in a dark cloak some color between green and black, and possessing beauty so fierce it took my breath away. Her eyes glittered like steel. She smiled in satisfaction as she disappeared. I felt my breathing deepen. Any and all strength drained from my limbs. Shaking my head and fighting to stay awake, I sank to the ground as I felt rushing winds in my ears and my senses whirled and then quieted all at once. My eyelids kept blinking. Maybe if I didn't let my lids close it wouldn't happen. But how could I stop them? They were so heavy. What if I died? What if the good fairy, Bernadette, had lied to us all? What if I didn't get my happily ever after? My eyelids were so very heavy. Rhythmically, methodically, I heard my gifts listed over and over inside my head. Almost like a chant.

She shall be given the gift of grace.
She shall be given the gift of beauty.
She shall be given the gift of song.
She shall be given the gift of creativity.
She shall be given the gift of delicacy.
She shall be given the gift of sweetness.

I think I felt a tear leave my eye, but my skin had started to feel so numb, I couldn't be sure. I saw blackness. It enfolded me in its heavy arms and took me away. I slept.

CHAPTER ONE

I felt life. It was strange, foreign. My limbs, my entire body tingled. Long since forgotten feelings and sensations rushed through my being. Darkness still surrounded me, but it was somehow less dark, less threatening. I struggled to open my eyes and it was with the great rushing of winds and roaring of oceans that I first again beheld light. It hurt my tender eyes and my mouth was dry and swollen. My tongue felt like a thick roll of felt, and goodness . . . I couldn't move. My limbs now felt frozen in place; helplessly stagnant from a century of inactivity. A century. A century! It was over. This had to be it. I blinked rapidly, trying to clear the fog from my eyes. My stomach lurched in anticipation and my heart stuttered within me.

Tentative, I looked around. I knew what I was looking for. If I was awake, somewhere around here was a man who was responsible and my nervousness threatened to overwhelm me. And then I saw him. A step or two away from my bed to the left of me stood a man. The man I suppose I had expected. Tall, slender yet strong, my rescuer stood mere feet from me. I squinted hard until my eyes came into focus.

And then my heart sputtered and nearly came to a full stop.

Never, *never* in all my waking sixteen years of life had I ever seen such a perfect man. His hair was the deepest, richest brown I could imagine and his eyes glittered silver, a seemingly mystic blend of steel and moonlight. As I stared deeper into his questioning gaze I noticed there were little flecks of green amid the metallic gray.

The silence between us became heavy and almost embarrassing. I realized with an uncomfortable jolt that I didn't know his side of this story. Had he known what would happen when he kissed me? My heart screeched to another halt as I made this connection in my brain. He had kissed me. Oh my. I was engaged. I smiled nervously, almost giddy.

The silence stretched on. The man's brow wrinkled. I had to say something. And quickly.

"Nnoshths tuuuhh mm—"

I stopped, horrified. Something was drastically wrong with my voice. I had a beautiful voice; singsong, trickling, musical, melodious even. But now I sounded like a fanatical witch hissing some dreadful curse. My breathing quickened as I fought panic again. As for my knight in shining armor, he looked positively alarmed. I tried again.

"Wsshpphhmmff," That sounded even worse.

"Wwwassthhher," I repeated it several times in varying attempts.

"Oh! Water," the man said, pulling out a canteen. His voice was a dream. I smiled again. Then, when it became awkwardly clear that I couldn't move my arms, he helped me prop up my head and poured the water into my mouth himself.

The water was a liquid cure. It coursed through me, rushing to bring relief to my parched body. I felt made anew. Turning my head toward the man, I gave him a real smile. I cleared my throat as daintily as I could and then began a speech I had rehearsed since I was six years old, trying to fall back on the confidence that had been pounded into me since birth.

"I am Princess Aurora Claire of Kalynbrae. But you may call me Claire. Everyone does. I am greatly beholden to you for rescuing me. Might I have the honor of inquiring my champion's name?" I tried my best to look sweet and pretty while praying that I didn't look as dusty as I felt.

My dashing rescuer knelt by my bedside and took my hand in his as he introduced himself as a Prince Damien from some kingdom called Gaël, which sounded vaguely familiar. I felt my heart flutter pleasantly. Alright. This was actually quite lovely. And it was just as I had always imagined and hoped it would be. Prince Damien was talking about how my beauty was beyond compare and I was more than he could have ever hoped for when some heavy object scraped against the floor and I turned to see another man. This didn't quite fit in my imaginings. The second man, practically a giant, was attempting to right a teetering armoire he'd apparently bumped into in his not so stealthy attempt to leave unnoticed.

"Who are you?" I asked, my voice still a little raspy.

"Oh, that's my companion, Sir James," Prince Damien explained turning my head with his hand back to himself. "He accompanied me on my quest to find you. Don't worry about him. He was just leaving."

Suddenly a great moan sounded. It grew in hoarse, scratchy eeriness until it sounded as though all the witches and gnomes and ogres in every storybook I had ever read had combined together to hiss in haunting unison. It quickly escalated into a hacking sort of cackle that shattered the stillness and caused all three of us to jump.

I leaped, well, stumbled really, from my bed, as well as could be expected after my hundred-year nap. My tower was to be guarded in quiet solitude by the coming generations in preparation for this very moment. Who could have possibly made all that noise? My prince and his companion drew their swords, ready to face any oncoming attacker.

I appreciated the chivalry, but I didn't quite feel afraid, which was sort of new for me. I was puzzled maybe, but not afraid. After all, this was my story. I knew it by heart. There was no monster to gobble me up after I'd survived so long in my deep sleep. The hard part had happened. That nightmare was over. Now was my happily ever. I was sure of it.

"Follow me," I entreated, boldly directing their weapons toward the ground and regally holding up my long white nightgown. A somewhat baffled Sir James opened the heavy door to my chamber and we walked out into the corridor.

The noise was nearly gone now, and as I glided purposefully ahead I stumbled over a large lump, falling flat on my face. A confused hustle of fabric flew out all over the place as my nightgown whooshed up around me and twisted with the limbs and clothing of the lump that had made me fall. Sir James and Prince Damien rushed to help me and we eventually straightened out the mess. I blushed furiously. Also, I couldn't remember ever tripping in my entire life and the mortification was excruciating. Even when obstacles had been in front of me, I had always neatly sidestepped them. I didn't have time to dwell on that however because I realized that the lump was actually a person and that person was a chambermaid who appeared to have fallen asleep right outside my door. I gasped as I realized she was not just any chambermaid. I knew her! I had seen her face hundreds of times. I searched my memory for her name. Amaline! That was it. She was having trouble talking and was hacking away so I asked Sir James to give her some water, which soon revived her.

"What happened, Your Highness?" she asked hoarsely, her eyes wide.

"It's the curse, Amaline!" I squealed. "It's over! I'm awake!" I gave her a quick hug. And then it dawned on me that she shouldn't actually be here. "Wait," I yelped, "Why are you even here at all?" She looked confused. "You're supposed to be dead," I tried to explain with a kind and patient smile. Now she looked terrified.

"What I mean is," I amended quickly. "It's been a hundred years. How can you possibly still be alive? And how can you look so young?" I was baffled.

"I'm afraid I really have no idea what is happening, Your Grace," Amaline's bottom lip quivered.

"Never mind, Amaline," I patted her shoulder. "Don't worry. We'll get this straightened out. I really am so happy you're alright." Unfortunately, I had no more time to console her further. An idea, a flicker of hope against hope was brimming up within me and I hardly dared entertain it until I investigated further. I rushed on. My hero and his attendant followed after me. We passed a squire who was coughing and rubbing his eyes. I recognized him. What was his name? Lyon? Theodore? And then I saw Sir Olivier, one of my father's most trusted knights. I bounded over to him and grasped his arm.

"Sir Olivier," I said, staring up at him, "How is this possible?"

He looked as confused as I felt and I motioned Sir James and his flask over to help the aging knight to some water. I had wasted enough time. Against my better judgment, yet unable to quell my growing excitement, I followed my swiftly moving feet toward my parents' quarters.

The huge wooden doors creaked eerily as I shoved my way past them. My father and mother were yawning and stretching on their enormous canopy bed. I could no longer hold back the tears that streamed down my face.

"Mama! Papa!" I yelled and leaped onto the mattress in between them.

"Claire!" they exclaimed simultaneously.

A good deal of hugging and kissing and crying and sighs of relief followed. No one knew what had happened or why the whole castle seemed to have fallen asleep along with me. Frankly, we didn't care. Eventually I remembered that we weren't alone and I delicately edged off of the bed and traipsed over to where Sir James and Prince Damien stood, awkwardly trying not to eavesdrop on our family reunion.

"Mother, Father, this is Prince Damien. And this is Sir James," I said, gesturing at each in their turn. "They are our rescuers."

My father, King Roland, quickly got out of bed and strode over to meet them.

"Thank you so much for everything you've done. We are indebted to you eternally." Prince Damien smiled and bowed gallantly while Sir James uncomfortably shifted his weight from one foot to the other and sort of bowed his head.

"Helen," my father motioned for my mother to join them, which she did, modestly clutching her lavender velvet robe to herself. He took her hand and kissed it tenderly before drawing her close to his side.

Prince Damien and Sir James bowed and my mother blushed. I think she was as overwhelmed by the prince's handsomeness as I was.

I joined the circle. "So, I guess this means that I'm betrothed. Right, Father?"

"Well, yes," he sputtered. "I suppose it does."

I turned to Prince Damien and extended my hand.

"Prince Damien." This was another speech I had practiced. "I am indeed indebted to you for freeing me . . . er—us from this curse. I offer myself as your reward. I shall consent to be your bride."

Sir James seemed to have some sort of coughing fit, but my prince looked pleased and that was all I cared about.

CHAPTER TWO

That night I tossed and turned restlessly in my bed. Not the same bed I'd been sleeping in for the last hundred years, thank goodness. This was my old bed. In my old room. The servants had made quick work of the dust and grime. It sparkled just as it had in the old days. I was relieved not to be up in that tower anymore. I'd asked mother and father to have it remodeled into some new room with a purpose other than housing an imprisoned and extremely sleepy princess. We had discussed it over supper. The palace hunters had been in a tizzy to shoot enough meat to feed everyone and although the meal was devoid of fresh vegetables, the cooks had concocted a surprisingly delicious meal. Everyone was is the mood to celebrate. Musicians played with exorbitant flare—the string players especially were in a grand mood seeing that their instruments had aged to a point of pricelessness and beauty— and there was a perpetual smile on everyone's face.

The feast went smoothly. Prince Damien seemed pleased with the food and gave me his undivided attention. The prince's companion, Sir James, looked ill at ease and almost pained by the fanfare. I couldn't understand what he found so distasteful. Perhaps we seemed old fashioned. It had been a hundred years, after all. But Prince Damien didn't seem annoyed and it hardly seemed polite to let any discomfort show. I didn't dwell on the matter long, however.

I was far too busy smiling and laughing and shyly gazing at Prince Damien from under my perfectly long, dark and curly lashes.

I opened those lashes now and gazed up at the top of my enormous four-poster bed. The canopy's normally lush blue-green color looked more like a shimmery gray in the darkness. I sighed, feeling hopeless. As my first ladies maid, and the closest thing I had ever had to a friend, Angeline had helped me prepare for bed I turned to her a bit apprehensively.

"Angeline, did you—" I stopped and bit my lip. "Do you remember the hundred years of sleeping? I mean, did it feel like it was a very long time?"

She stopped brushing my hair and looked thoughtful.

"I suppose not, Your Highness. To me, it seemed like it was only yesterday that I was with . . ." she trailed off and blinked rapidly.

I knew of her relationship with Alvere, of course, although not in much detail. We were close enough to have swapped romantic stories, but she was discreet and I had never had any. I was well aware of her engagement, however. I also knew that her fiancé was still unaccounted for.

"I'm sure he'll turn up," I tried to sound confident.

"I'm afraid not, Your Highness," she bit back a little sob. "He had been sent out on an errand by the head stable master. I don't think he was within the palace walls."

I didn't know what to say. I only knew I felt miserable for her. This was, after all, mostly my fault.

"I'm sorry," she sniffed. "I shouldn't be bothering you with this. This is a happy time. With your handsome prince come to rescue you." She smiled at me and I smiled back but quickly looked away. I couldn't shake the feeling of guilt that clung to me, clawing its way uncomfortably into my stomach.

She'd left me with one candle burning and I kept it lit long after she'd gone.

Darkness made me nervous. It never had before. I tried to examine my feelings. I didn't think it had felt like a hundred years. It hadn't felt like a mere moment either though. It felt like one of those nights where you have dream after dream, none of them pleasant. The kind of night that seemed to go on forever.

I had dreamed of memories, but they were never complete or exact. There was always a detail I couldn't recall or some aspect that was unclear. I remember the agonizing effort of trying to grasp those details and feeling as though I was constantly pulling my fingers through hazy air. The most vivid dream was the one where I relived my last memory. I would see myself as though from another point of view as I hypnotically climbed the stairs to that foreboding tower and walked toward the spinning wheel until I reached out and slowly touched that needle, pressing until it drew blood. Then I'd see myself look at the old woman. She always transformed into her true self. I knew her name just as I knew all parts of my story. Zora, Queen of the Dark Fairies. But her face was unclear. I could never quite summon the image to the front of my mind. She was hidden deep inside the recesses of my mind. But whether that was by her or by my own willpower I didn't know.

I knew I would never be able to sleep with the direction my thoughts had taken. For a moment I wondered if I'd ever be able to sleep again. It all used to seem so simple. I never considered how I'd feel once the sleep was over. I'd never realized how threatening normal, nightly sleep would seem after that. I sank down onto my window seat and stared at the way the moonlight cast a metallic sheen onto the swaying trees and long stalks of grass, looking for the romance. Looking for the exciting spin I could throw on the scene. It wasn't working. Not at night. Not in the dark. I knew in my head that the sleep was over, but my heart kept asking, *If you fall asleep again, how do you know you'll ever wake up?*

My eyes flew open and my head fell backward and hit the wall. I'd dozed off while sitting in my window alcove. Early daylight streamed onto my face. I'd woken up. I took deep breaths as I tried to figure out how much sleep I'd actually gotten. Not much, I was sure. I felt dizzy as I wandered over to my mirror. No dark circles. Hair perfectly in place. A healthy flush in my cheeks. Fortunately for me and my fairy gifts, no one would ever know how exhausted I was.

But I *had* woken up.

And I hadn't had any nightmares. That relieved my fears to some degree. Perhaps tonight I'd be able to get more of a full night's rest. Angeline bustled in followed closely by Corrinne and Annette. They prettied me up with minimal effort. I really think they had the easiest job in the palace. Thank you, good fairy number two. The gift of beauty came in handy after a night of little to no sleep. I yawned and finally realized there was a hint of excitement in the air.

"Why are you three so animated this morning?" I asked.

"Oh, it's nothing, Princess," Angeline smiled as she flounced my skirt for me. I wore a deep rose satin gown that complemented my eyes and skin tone. The bodice cinched my waist in tightly and the close fitting sleeves stopped at my elbow. The skirt parted in the front to reveal a cream colored under layer. I had wanted to wear my blue gown. I shrugged my shoulders and turned away from the looking glass.

"It's just that it's everyone's first morning after . . ." Annette petered to a stop.

"Oh yes, of course," I agreed brightly, ignoring her awkwardness. "It certainly is wonderful to have things back to normal." Normal? What was normal? What did a day post-curse look like?

"What is on the schedule for today?" I asked, trying to establish a sense of calm in myself. It felt so strange to be going about my duties as though nothing had happened. The impending doom known to us simply as "the curse" or "the sleep" had always cast a shadow of predictability on all my actions. Occasionally I had slipped into moods where I thought nothing much mattered. I was simply passing time. Usually when that happened I wrote stories or created paintings of my future to cheer myself out of my complacency. The colors in this future were brighter. I was blissfully happy. And my prince, although his eye and hair color changed depending on my age and passing fancies, was handsome and kind.

Initially, my parents had struggled with deciding if they should tell me my fate or not. They went back and forth with the pros and cons of the situation. They struggled whether or not to let me know that everyone I cared about would die before I reached seventeen years old. Before I had even begun to do anything with my life. In the end, they let my growing personality be their guide. I was cheerful and positive. They thought I would be able to handle it. So they decided to tell me. But they didn't just *tell* me. They told me *over* and *over*. They decided complete transparency would be best. Or rather, a very romanticized version of transparency. I heard my story told in song. I saw it performed out by the finest play actors. I listened to it as a bedtime story. I believe there was even a ballet choreographed at some point. Even with my tutors, I recited the facts of it as if it were a glorious event in our history. Only I was learning my future. I know it was hard for my parents to hear, each and every time. I remember glancing over at them only to see their plastered-on, brave smiles beaming back at me. So I'd put on a brave smile myself. Mirroring their farce as best I could.

When I was seven, I realized that I was the only child to whom this would ever happen. I threw a bit of a fit at that. It wasn't much of one. I had the gift of sweetness, you see. My unpleasantness never lasted too long. Whether I liked it or not. But my fate had seemed completely unfair to me. In an effort to smooth my ruffled feathers, my tutors rushed to inform me that this made me special and impor-tant. I was to be a brave and glorious pioneer, filled to the brim with admirable, fairy-given traits as I marched, or rather glided, into my enchanted future. I was a wonder, they'd said.

"—and then there's the ball this evening." Angeline's voice star-tled me out of my reverie.

My face brightened instantly, almost as though it had a will of its own. Yesterday my father had announced a ball in celebration of what we were all calling "the awakening." I could hardly contain my excitement. I loved dancing and was quite good at it, thanks, once again, to my fairy gifts. It was even rumored that my graceful turns and quick footwork was praised as reminiscent to the great fairy Tressla's own skills on a dance floor. Both happy and nervous, I gave myself a final once-over in the mirror before bidding my ladies in waiting farewell and making my way over to the breakfast hall.

After scanning the room quickly, I found my mother and father sitting at the head of the long dining table. Their heads were bent together as they cooed and giggled together, holding hands like young sweethearts. I smiled ruefully. For as long as I could remember my parents had been this way. It was part of the reason I had so much faith in my happily ever after. I'd seen a happily ever after play out in front of me my entire life. I joined my parents at my seat after giving them each an enthusiastic kiss on the cheek.

"How did you sleep, my darling?" my mother asked as she unfolded a satin napkin and placed it on her lap.

"Um, fine," I hemmed, busying myself with my own napkin so I wouldn't have to look either of them in the eye. I hated lying, but I didn't want to worry them with my fears.

"Don't worry, sweet," my father said as he patted my hand. "You'll soon adjust. It's to be expected that there might be some trepidation or anxiety on your part. It was a strange experience for all of us—going to sleep for the first time since . . . well, since we all woke up."

"Was it?" I asked eagerly. "Was it hard to fall asleep?" I was simultaneously worried about them suffering last night and relieved that I might not have been the only one.

"Well, I must confess, I felt a moment's unrest about the whole thing, but I was simply so overwhelmed from the events of the day I quickly fell asleep and slept like a log all night." My mother said this as she examined and then flicked away a minuscule piece of lint on my father's sleeve.

"Oh," I looked away, feeling terribly guilty that I was not completely happy about the fact that my mother had had a peaceful night's rest.

"Everything will get back to normal now and we can move on with our lives. Don't worry," my mother smiled at me.

There was that word again. *Normal.* What did that even mean? How was I supposed to get back to something that I'd never known? I swallowed my questions and smiled back at her. Just then, Sir James entered the room, very hesitantly and looking extremely uncomfortable. As usual.

"Sir James," my father's voice boomed as he smiled broadly and motioned for the knight to join us at the table. "You are very welcome this morning. I hope your rooms were comfortable."

"Yes, very," Sir James acknowledged with a slight bob of the head. "Thank you, Your Majesty."

"Where is Prince Damien?" my mother asked, more for my benefit than for hers.

"He's—he'll join us shortly," Sir James answered.

I watched him sit and glance uneasily at the sumptuous spread before us. With nothing else to do I took the opportunity to examine him more closely. Since he was normally accompanied by Prince Damien, who captivated all my attention, I don't think I'd yet really looked at him beyond a cursory glance. He was tall, for one thing. Well, that was an understatement. He stood nearly a full head taller than the prince and his shoulders were extremely broad and forbidding looking. He looked like he belonged outdoors where things were wide and open, as though being indoors made him cramped and pinched. His honey-colored hair started to curl just as it curved above his ears. The few glimpses of his eyes I'd had revealed them to be a deep blue. They were large eyes that had a pleasant, round openness to them. His nose was straight and his mouth was twisted into an uncomfortable grimace at the moment. His jaw clenched as he shifted in his seat, waiting for Prince Damien to make his appearance.

As if on cue, Prince Damien entered a moment later, looking resplendent and well rested. I hadn't thought it possible, but he somehow looked even more handsome than he had yesterday.

"Good morning," he said as he smiled at all of us and walked with purpose over to take the seat next to mine.

"Good morning," my mother and father returned in unison. I simply smiled and blushed.

"I trust you all slept well," Damien said as the servants began bringing in trays full of steaming buns, cold meats, and fresh fruits. I again said nothing, so that I wouldn't have to lie. I noticed Sir James said nothing as well. He had dark circles under his eyes now that I looked more closely. He glanced up and caught me staring at him.

I quickly looked away in embarrassment. I began eating the sliced and peeled peach that one of the servants had placed in front of me. Apparently our orchards had fared well in their years of wildness. The juices dripped down my chin. Surprised at an unprecedented show of indelicacy, I quickly dabbed it away with my napkin.

My father started outlining the plan for the day. There was a lot of legislative and administrative work to be done in councils, which Prince Damien was expected to attend. He acquiesced graciously and winked at me when my father made a joke about how that would leave less time for him to spend time with me. I didn't wink back, but I smiled my most beguiling smile. Then we discussed plans for the ball that would take place that evening. Tonight my father would announce my engagement formally to our court as well as the new treaty and alliance terms with Prince Damien's kingdom, which now encompassed all of ours as well, since it had been left ungoverned after the great sleep came. Prince Damien responded enthusiastically about participating in the councils and about his excitement for the ball. His exuberance was contagious and I felt my spirits lift higher and higher with each word he spoke.

CHAPTER THREE

$\mathcal{G}$oodbye for now, Princess Aurora," Prince Damien said as he winked again and left a quick kiss on my hand. We had finished breakfast and we all went our separate ways. Prince Damien joined my father and his advisors, my mother left to discuss ball preparations with the palace staff, and Sir James went off on his own to who knows where. That left me to my own devices, and I quickly headed over to the stables. I'd rushed to greet my cherished horse Naomi yesterday, but with all the hustle I'd had no time to ride. I greeted the stable hands, Alvin and Theo, brightly and they quickly saddled Naomi and brought her to me.

"Hello, old friend." My forehead pressed close to her nose as she whinnied softly and bobbed her head up and down in anticipation. Theo placed the mounting block and then assisted me onto the saddle. Taking off through the large doors and out into the open air, I rode leisurely through the gardens, observing how run down they'd become during the curse. There was hardly a hint of the former glory my mother took such pride in. Many gardeners smiled and waved as they worked to make some sense of the gnarled mess. Once past the gardens I nudged Naomi so she picked up the pace. We fell into a gentle gallop as I rode over a bridge and through a wide field toward the woods. These woods had been within the palace walls and were kept pretty well manicured; well, at least they used to be. Nudging

Naomi with my knees, I raced through the trees. I felt my hair fall from its pins and tumble down my back and I shook it out, grinning as I relished the sensation of wind rushing past me. My target location loomed in the distance and I pulled back slightly on the reigns to slow Naomi's pace. One of my favorite places in these woods was this pond. It was small and mossy. It always seemed to have a gently clinging fog creeping over it, which cast an air of mystery to the spot. I swung my leg over Naomi to dismount and I led her closer to the water. The trees overhead were close and blocked out much of the sunlight. One of my favorite things to do was to look up at the green canopy above me and watch how the light sparkled behind those leaves, leaving speckles of light dancing on the surface of everything around me. I sat gingerly on a slab of rock, careful not to muddy my dress. Leaves and twigs snapped from somewhere behind me and I whirled to see what had caused the interruption. Sir James glanced up just as I turned to see him, and he appeared as startled as I felt. For a moment we simply stared at each other in bewilderment. I saw that he led his horse behind him.

"Princess Aurora, I'm sorry," he stammered. "I was riding and I spotted this pond. I thought I might water my horse."

I was suddenly aware that my hair was unbound and I struggled to tame it into a braid as I stood to face him completely, realizing after only about a second that I had no idea how to braid my own hair. I dropped my hands back to my sides with a blush and bit my lip.

"No need to apologize, Sir James," I said. "You merely startled me. That's all. I'm not used to anyone else coming here, but of course it's free to use."

"Thank you," he smiled. I think this was the first time I'd seen him smile. It was a smallish, polite smile, but a smile nonetheless. He seemed much more at ease outside in the fresh air than he did within the walls of the castle. Smiling back, tentatively, I nodded. He walked past me with his horse to the water's edge. We both shifted our weight from one foot to another a little awkwardly.

"Well, I should be getting back," I said with a shrug. There was nothing that I needed to get back for, but we didn't seem to have much to talk about and I had come here to be alone after all.

"I'm sorry again for intruding. I won't be long. You can stay and enjoy your peace here if you wish." Sir James was apologetic.

"Oh, don't worry. I was just revisiting some of my old haunts. Enjoy your ride," I bowed my head slightly in farewell and he did the same. There was another brief awkward instant where he seemed unsure of whether he should offer to help me onto my horse. Didn't he know he should offer to help?

"I, um," I began. "Would you assist me onto my horse?"

"Oh, of course," he mumbled. He found a rock and dragged it over to my horse with what I considered alarming ease considering how big the rock was. He took my hand and helped me use the stone as a mounting block. I thanked him quickly and he started to move away.

"Well, I'll see you later," I said in parting.

He simply nodded his agreement.

And with that, our strange exchange ended and I rode quickly away. Relieved to be on my own again, I rode for another hour, exploring the grounds and checking in on other favorite places. They were all surprisingly less altered than I'd feared and I was delighted with the familiarity I found.

I reached my rooms a little before midday and Angeline summoned a few maids to help with my hair. It untangled easily and they wound it back into the low, twisted bun that they had created this morning. Angeline arranged the delicate curls around my face and told me the wind had put a becoming flush in my cheeks. At this we all giggled. Everyone knew I always had a becoming flush in my cheeks.

Word came that the advisory councils were taking longer than expected so the midday meal would be served privately in our rooms. I ate absentmindedly, thinking of when I might see Prince Damien again. Before long it was time to prepare for the ball and several handmaids again surrounded me as they dressed me in an elegant gown of pale aquamarine. The rich satin clung to me in all the right places and the deep blue accent silk accentuated my turquoise eyes perfectly. I wore a diamond pendant around my neck, and glittering earrings trailed down my neck. My hair became a glorious concoction of curls, twists, and braids. I spun slowly in front of the mirror to the admiring sighs of my maids. I thanked them profusely and walked out of my room to join my parents before entering the ball.

Damien tugged gently on my arm to lead me into the ballroom. I felt my stomach jump, but I couldn't tell if it was from his touch or the excitement of entering the glamorously decorated hall. I glanced sideways at my companion. He was above average height, but only just. He was several inches taller than I, which allowed me a satisfactory view of his finely crafted facial features. His high cheekbones led to full lips, which seemed permanently fixed in a saucy, roguish grin. I thought again of his kiss, or rather the fact that I regrettably couldn't remember it, and I felt my face warm. He chose that exact moment to look back at me. I cleared my throat and glanced away, but he just laughed and pulled me a bit closer. Once we reached the dance floor, the crowd stilled and the orchestra conductor tapped his baton to begin the first waltz. Damien took me confidently into his arms and began dancing. Thank goodness for my gift of gracefulness because I would have stumbled all over his perfectly shaped feet in my nervousness. His movements were smooth and fluid. He somehow managed to turn a relatively prudish dance into something that made me blush again simply by the way that he looked at me. Halfway through the dance, one of my father's chancellors tapped him on the shoulder.

"I'm so sorry to interrupt, Prince Damien, but we have some urgent questions for you."

Damien looked mildly irritated, but recovered quickly when he saw Sir James walking by. He waved him over and then turned back to me.

"I hate to leave you, but duty demands my attention yet again. I'll be back as soon as I can." By then Sir James had reached us.

"Have a dance with her, will you, James?" Damien grinned and with a wink, walked smoothly away with the chancellor. I swallowed my disappointment and turned to smile politely at Sir James when I noticed his face had become an even more pronounced mask of discomfort and dread. Hardly flattering. Must this man constantly be displeased? What could he possibly have to be unhappy about?

"Thank you so much for stepping in," I smiled gratefully. "I'd hate to be left here all alone on the dance floor."

"Of course, Your Highness," he replied dutifully.

I was surprised at his deft footwork and relatively graceful presence considering his size. He confidently guided me through every turn and sweep of the dance, but his face remained distant and uncomfortable. I was not accustomed to such treatment and in my annoyance I forgot my manners and stared at him in puzzled frustration. As soon as the music stopped he propelled me toward one of my attendants and vanished after a curt bow.

"Well, of all the strange, rude—" my muttering was cut off by the appearance of Damien.

"So sorry, Aurora, darling. I came back as soon as I could get away. I trust James was accommodating?" I was too distracted by the casual yet wonderful way he called me "darling" to respond coherently.

"What? James? Sir James?" I stammered, "Oh yes, he was charming. You know, you really can call me Claire. My parents do. It's what everyone who really knows me calls me."

Damien chuckled as he took my hand and placed it in the crook of his elbow.

"But Aurora is so beautiful, so delicate and elegant—just like what it means. You are a beautiful dawn. A soft sunrise." He led me to the dance floor and we again joined the dancing couples on the floor.

"Yes, of course, but Claire is light, transparency, illumination . . . Also, beautiful?" I bit my lip.

"Of course," Damien smiled indulgently and before I could say more we began a lively dance that left little time for conversation. As soon as the music stopped, my father's high chancellor stood to announce the king's declaration.

"All hail King Roland! Long live the king!" The attendees echoed the sentiment and my father stepped up to the front of the room.

"My loyal subjects, it gives me great pleasure to announce the betrothal of my daughter, Princess Aurora Claire, to Prince Damien of Gaël." The audience erupted into applause and calls of encouragement and approval. My father continued, "It also pleases me to inform you that after careful deliberation and consideration, an alliance between our fair kingdom and Gaël shall be established forthwith and the original boundaries of our respective kingdoms will return to what they once were, although under a joint rule, with Prince Damien and Princess Aurora Claire as heirs to the entire kingdom." More applause and appreciative noises ensued and I smiled up at Damien adoringly. He returned my smile and squeezed my hand. The dancing soon recommenced and Damien whisked me back into the whirling circle of dancers. I saw my parents dancing and looking at each other with love in their eyes nearby. I laughed with delight and found myself feeling happier than I could ever remember being.

Later on, I stood near the refreshment table as Damien spoke with several courtiers who were eager to hear about how things had changed in the last century. I spotted Sir James standing alone near an archway that led out onto the balcony. His shoulders were slumped and I began to take pity on him. After a moment's hesitation, and a quick glance to see that Damien was thoroughly engrossed in his conversation and probably would be for a while, I walked over to where Sir James stood, facing away from me.

"It's been a lovely ball, don't you think?" I asked him from behind. He turned in surprise.

"Um, yes, I suppose so." He hesitated and nodded as though trying to dismiss me.

My brow furrowed and I tried not to roll my eyes.

"Have you not enjoyed yourself? Is the food or music not to your liking?"

"No, no, everything is very . . . elegant," he assured disinterestedly.

I was about to walk away in defeat when he muttered something I couldn't make out, but the tone left little to the imagination. Fed up with his attitude, I whirled back around and placed my hands on my hips.

"What is the matter with you?" I demanded in frustration, "We have done nothing but try to make you feel at home since you arrived and this is how you act in return for such kindness?"

He barked out a short laugh and shook his head.

"Me? Feel at home?"

What was wrong with this man? Was Prince Damien's kingdom really so much more luxurious that our palace seemed like a peasant's hut to him? Damien didn't seem to think so. Or at least he didn't let it affect his manners.

"You really are the most insufferable snob," I scowled and then my eyes widened in horror and I threw a hand over my mouth. I didn't think I had ever said anything that rude in my life. Where on earth was my sweetness?

Sir James's looked surprised and rushed to explain. "No, I didn't mean—what I meant was that I don't belong here. I don't —" He stopped talking abruptly.

"It doesn't matter what I think," he stated and bowed before walking briskly away.

I was going to let him go. What did it matter what one knight thought of our kingdom? Then again, no one had really ever disapproved of anything I'd done and I didn't like the feeling. I glanced behind me to see that Damien was still laughing and chatting with the group of courtiers and felt sure I wouldn't be missed for only a few moments. I gathered up my long, full skirt in my hands and delicately hurried after Sir James.

He was about to enter the terrace through an archway in a darkened alcove so I quickly moved through another archway just to my right and cut him off abruptly.

"Why don't you like me?" I demanded boldly. James's mouth twitched in disbelieving laughter before he shook his head and looked away in irritation. I couldn't understand the amusement. I was genuinely perplexed. I couldn't remember the last time someone didn't like me. What wasn't to like? I was *made* to be likeable.

"What I mean is why do you seem to hate me? You don't even know me," I tried clarifying.

James extended his arms and rested his hands in front of him on the marble railing.

"I don't think one less admirer will make much difference, Your Highness, so why does it matter?"

"What is *that* supposed to mean?"

He let his eyes perform an exaggerated appraisal of my person before looking back out at the view as if his action explained everything.

Annoyingly, I flushed (delicacy, you know). Well, of course I was beautiful and graceful and all of those feminine traits. I was used to being admired for these things. I was unaccustomed to being shunned and despised for them. Not even the other girls had faulted me for being prettier than they were. They knew my beauty came with a price that they were unwilling to pay. None of them wanted to prick their finger and fall asleep for a hundred years. After all, it wasn't my fault I was this way. It had just simply always . . . been. I couldn't stand that he made me feel bad for being the way I was when really, I had never had anything to do with it.

"This is just how I am," my explanation sounded pathetic, even to my own ears. "I mean, I was made this way. I—I was given these things. I didn't ask for them." I knew I was making it worse. But I didn't know how to explain what I felt.

"It's not my fault," I tried once more to clarify, but I felt tears sting my eyes. Surprised and angry, I blinked them away. I turned quickly on my heel and left before Sir James could say anything else.

Reentering the ballroom, I pasted on a smile and looked for Damien. I found him right where I had left him and I hurried to his side.

"Aurora, darling," he turned to me with a smile. "I was just wondering where you'd wandered off to."

I guess *Aurora* was going to stick.

"Just thought I'd get a breath of fresh air," I said nonchalantly. "It's a bit warm in here."

"Isn't it?" he agreed.

The courtiers bowed and made their excuses before walking off in different directions.

"So," Damien smirked. "One last dance before the evening's through?"

"Of course," I answered readily, finding that my smile was once again genuine.

We joined the other couples and enjoyed a spirited dance around the floor. Afterwards, I bade my parents and Damien an exhausted adieu before going with Angeline and Yvette in the direction of my rooms. The day had been tiring and my lack of sleep the night before was catching up with me. I sat docilely while my maids removed my gown, slipped my nightgown over my head, and brushed through my hair.

"Good night, Princess," Angeline smiled at me before quietly leaving and closing the door behind her.

I sank into the silky sheets of my soft and warm bed. My tired head dropped gratefully onto my pillow. I shut my eyes.

All I could see was the needle. My eyes flew open and I gasped. I tried closing them again and I saw a drop of blood. My blood.

"Not again," I moaned. I tried several more times, but it was no use. The images my mind produced were too frightening to ignore. I sighed in resignation and got out of bed. Wearily, I tied a long velvet robe around my body and pushed my hair to the side. My bedroom door slid open with a minimal amount of noise and I slipped silently out into the hall. These corridors were so familiar to me I could have found my way with my eyes closed and I knew how to reach the east terrace without being detected by any guards. Perhaps a bit of cool night air would refresh me. I pushed all thoughts of fear from my mind and concentrated on the present. The hallway was dark, but the glow from the moonlight coming through windows high above my head was enough to slightly illuminate my reflection in the tall mirrors as I walked by. I paused for a moment before one of them and examined myself closely.

If it has not already been made abundantly clear, I am someone very well acquainted with her own appearance. My father and mother had extravagantly placed mirrors around nearly every corner in the palace. No long passageway was lacking. Each room had at least one wall-sized monstrosity and smaller vanity-sized glasses were peppered throughout the entire palace. I think they meant it to be kind. I believe in their minds they saw these mirrors as a reminder of the good that had come from my fairy blessings. It was as if they wanted me to always remember that although I must "die," in a manner of speaking, at only sixteen, at least I was beautiful, graceful, and the list goes on. As a result, I know every line, curve, and contour of my face by heart. I could create an exact replica of myself in any medium: stone, fresco, canvas, bronze, without so much as one peep in the mirror—of course that might also have to do with the fact that, thanks to another fairy gift, I possess more artistic ability in my little finger than most artisans have in their entire bodies. My face now looked as it always did. Perfect on the surface, but I could see the anxiousness beneath. I sighed and kept going, turning a blind eye to the never-ending parade of mirrors as I walked on.

CHAPTER FOUR

I walked out of the large archway leading to the terrace quietly, hoping not to disturb anyone. Moonlight coated the cool marble and dark green ivy that hedged up and around the banisters and columns. I sighed in contentment as I sank onto a smooth bench and rested my elbows on the railing in front of me. My chin found its way into my warm palms as I looked at the impressive view before me. Although very run down, my father's palace grounds maintained their majestic dignity. My surroundings looked very much as I had left them, only wilder and more reckless, like the gardens and the woods I had ridden through that morning. With the glaze of shimmering moonlight, I found I preferred it that way. This dark sky and glittering starlight made everything beautiful. Different, but beautiful. *Everything* was different. All because of a kiss. I thought again of that kiss and I felt my cheeks flush. I brought my forehead down into my hands blocking out the scene that had been so pleasing only moments before. I had not anticipated the awkwardness and discomfort of this situation. Everyone was awake now because someone had kissed me. And everyone knew it.

I had never been kissed before. Although admired by men everywhere for my attractive arsenal of fairy-gifted attributes, I had lived a somewhat sequestered life. Not to mention no one was very interested in getting attached to someone who was already spoken for, even if I was spoken for by someone who wouldn't be born for many decades. Therefore, having had no personal experience, I had relied on what my mother told me. She always said that kisses were magical. When my father kissed her they had both fallen under a beautiful spell of love. When I cried she soothed me with magical kisses of comfort on my young face. She promised me that a magical kiss would save me. I grew to have faith in kisses. I believed they were powerful. I just didn't know how embarrassing it would be to have everyone I knew be party to my first one.

A quiet cough to my right made me snap my head up and I jumped in surprise. Sir James stood a few feet away.

"I'm sorry to startle you," he rushed to explain, "I just thought that something might be wrong . . . Um . . . you were so still."

"Don't apologize," I said awkwardly. "I'm fine."

After he hadn't gone anywhere for nearly a full minute and the silence became too heavy to bear, I gestured to the space next to me on the bench in invitation. He hesitatingly sat. The size of the bench combined with the bulk of his broad shoulders caused our arms to brush just slightly. He certainly was a large man . . . or rather, young man . . . or, what was he actually? He was tall enough and strong enough to be a fully matured man without question, but he had the face of someone younger, little more than a youth. Or at least there was the remnant of such a face. In closer proximity I detected a few lines around his eyes and mouth that suggested a hardness or bitterness that I had not noticed before. He looked weary in a way that made me sad, although I was not sure why. I think he sensed my peripheral appraisal because he nervously turned his head in my direction before returning to look out straight ahead.

"We really must stop meeting this way," I joked, trying to lighten the mood. He smiled in surprise before looking away from me again.

"Can't sleep?" he asked.

"It would appear so," I answered.

"It's been . . . an eventful couple of days. I'm sure you have a lot on your mind."

"Yes . . ." He seemed to have a gift for stating the obvious. His hands began to fidget nervously. We could both sense the tension that remained between us since our last meeting. I sighed and decided to take pity on him and keep the conversation going. My annoyingly adamant gifts seemed to insist upon it.

"What about you? Why aren't you sleeping?"

He considered my question and then shrugged. "I guess it's been a long few days for everyone."

When I didn't say anything he continued.

"We, the prince and I, have been searching for this place for so long, it's strange to think that it is all over now." He paused for a moment. "It makes me wonder what will happen next."

"Don't you live in Prince Damien's Court? Won't you just return home and resume your normal duties?" I asked.

A strange look came over his face, but I couldn't pinpoint the emotion I saw there. He seemed suddenly restless. He rose and took the short step toward the balcony. Leaning down, he rested his forearms on the marble railing in front of him. Then, eventually, he spoke.

"Yes, yes. I'm sure I'll just simply be able to return home." His sarcastic tone puzzled me. Maybe the thought of inactivity or lack of definite purpose frightened him. Maybe the end of a long journey posed more uncertainty than the start. I could certainly relate to that. I stood up and matched his pose. I felt inexplicably closer to him and suddenly decided to share something.

"I'm afraid too."

He glanced at me in surprise.

"What?"

"I'm afraid to fall asleep because . . . well, because I'm afraid I won't wake back up." I blinked rapidly to stop the foolish tears that pricked my eyes. "I know that must sound ridiculous." Hearing it out loud certainly made it sound that way to me. "I know sleeping must seem the least threatening thing in the world. I don't know why I should be so . . ." I realized I was nervously babbling and stopped, biting my lip and looking away swiftly.

He didn't say anything, for which I was grateful, yet at the same time disappointed. He didn't touch me either; any knight would have been far too polite and aware of social boundaries to do that.

But he shifted his weight ever so slightly so that his shoulder moved a fraction of an inch closer to mine. I sniffed and we stood there silently, watching the moon cast her glittering shadows while a lone night breeze dried the solitary tear from my face.

I was twelve years old. I waltzed through the corridors toward my dancing lesson. My tread was light and I executed spin after spin. Most likely I'd end up giving my teachers a few pointers like I had last week. Like I did most weeks. It embarrassed me a little the first few times my teachers had realized I had a tighter turn and quicker step than they did, but I had grown accustomed to it. The dancing lessons really did seem a bit pointless, but they helped pass the time. A muffled giggle somewhere ahead of me caused me to stop and listen, curious. I inched closer to the sound and peeked around a corner. Two young ladies stood close together, their heads nearly touching as they spoke rapidly in hushed tones. I heard a few snippets about some young man who had recently been knighted in my father's court. He was indeed handsome, if you like that sort. Of course I didn't know if I did. My future intended's looks were a complete mystery to me. I liked to imagine different varieties of faces, coloring, height, build, and so forth. But it changed nearly every time I thought about him. The two girls looked mischievous and happy. Something in my heart ached to be a part of the silly whispering. I took a deep breath and stepped toward them, clearing my throat daintily as I did. The girls started and looked up at me. Then they both smiled and curtsied. There was no animosity there, yet there was no closeness either.

"Good morning, Your Highness," they said in unison.

"Good morning," I answered.

"Are you on your way to your dance lesson?" one of them asked. I thought her name was Giselle.

"Yes, I am."

"I'm sure you don't even need it, you dance so superbly," the other gushed.

"Thank you," I blushed. I wanted to talk about something else, something that friends would talk about, but I was at a loss. Both girls looked at the ground after a moment of awkward silence.

"Well," I said brightly. "I must be going. Have a lovely day."

"And the same to you, Your Highness."

They were very kind. Nothing in their manners was wanting. So why did I feel so snubbed? So looked over? I squared my shoulders and continued on to my lesson.

When I woke up the following morning, I again wasn't sure how long I had slept. Maybe an hour? Possibly two? Sir James and I had parted shortly after my somewhat embarrassing revelation and several long minutes of comfortable and then increasingly awkward silence. I had wandered the corridors a bit more before finally returning to my room to stare at the stars from my window. At some point I must have fallen into bed in exhaustion, but I couldn't remember it. I stumbled blindly to my vanity and sat with my eyes still closed until Yvette came to assist me in getting ready with an explanation that Angeline was busy this morning. As I heard her approach I turned to her sleepily and dragged my eyes open. What I saw was a horrified expression on the stunned woman's face and a swift intake of breath. She clasped her hands over her mouth and ran out of the room.

That seemed . . . odd.

I turned slowly toward my mirrors and fought to see clearly. I jolted in my seat when I noticed something amiss. I squinted as hard as I could and leaned toward the mirror. My mouth dropped open in dumbfounded astonishment.

I now knew why Yvette had run out of the room.

I had to stifle a horrified shriek of my own.

I squinted. I scrunched my face. I turned away and then quickly back again. Nothing helped.

I had three distinct freckles right on the bridge of my nose.

It only got worse after that. Angeline forced Yvette to come back and help me get ready. A fine covering of beauty powder was applied to my nose to cover the spots, but the foreign substance made me sneeze and it had to be reapplied twice. The worst came when she had to brush my hair. We both shuddered when she encountered her first tangle. Her hands shook and she steadied herself on the back of my chair. I bit my lip as she gently tugged on a snarl. Having never experienced this type of pain before, I couldn't completely blink back the tears that formed in my stinging eyes. We both ended up sobbing and my maid had to be replaced three times before we got through all of my hair.

Once the ordeal of getting ready was finally over, I called for a light breakfast to be brought to my room. I would have been terribly late to the dining hall once I was finally presentable anyway. After nibbling at the bread and fruits on my tray a bit distractedly, I wandered over to the window and saw Damien and Sir James walking down below. They were talking enthusiastically as they strode toward the stables. Laughter burst forth from Damien as he playfully shoved James's shoulder. Even caught off guard and mid-stride, James's form barely acknowledged the push. No doubt if he had returned the action Damien would have staggered. That thought made me feel very disloyal. I quickly tuned my attention to Damien's finer points. His dark hair's devastating shine that could be seen all the way from my window. His bright laughter. James hadn't returned the laugh or the push. These two men seemed like such complete opposites. Damien was carefree, witty, charismatic, and stylish while James was subdued, quiet, and towering. My careful assessment of the two men was interrupted by Angeline's voice.

"It's nice to see such good friends, isn't it?"

"Mmm," I said noncommittally. I said no more and she bustled toward the door.

I observed them until they disappeared into the stables. This business of friendship was fascinating to me. Probably because real, true friendship had always eluded me. My gifts had made me intimidating and the fact that none of these people had assumed they would be around a hundred years from now made everyone a bit distant and uninterested. The combination resulted in very few friendships. Angeline and I were close, but she had always kept up a wall that meant she knew her place as my lady in waiting. I was well enough liked by everyone I met; my fairy-endowed personality was too gracious and pleasing to allow anyone to really hate me. I think even jealous girls and heartbroken admirers liked me against their wills. But the liking never resulted in or progressed to anything deeper or more meaningful. Even the relationships I shared with my mother and father had always had some strain. I suppose they felt they should have protected me better from the curse, which of course is silly since fairies will do whatever they please and my fate was something completely out of their power. But the fact had remained. They would lose me at sixteen. Although I considered them my only true friends, there was always a nagging in the back of my mind that only after my sleep could I find real friends—when at last no one would expect me to simply pause my existence for a hundred years. But that day was here. Would it happen now? What if it didn't? What would be my excuse then?

CHAPTER FIVE

y morning had made me somber. Seeking to find the positive, to regain my initial excitement upon waking up, I reflected on my progress with Sir James. Since our mostly silent meeting the night before, it seemed that James and I had come to some kind of understanding. Where we had been at first suspiciously civil, then irritably dismissive, we were now calmly accepting of each other's presence. At our midday meal he avoided my gaze until I finally caught his eye and gave him a small smile of apology and forgiveness all rolled into one. He responded by nodding his head almost imperceptibly and softening the rigid line of his shoulders. It was a start.

As soon as we finished eating I followed Damien eagerly outside so he could introduce me to his horse. He took my hand and placed it in the crook of his arm.

"You'll love Cosan," he said, smiling at me, "And of course he'll adore you too."

"Well . . . I, um, I certainly hope so," I responded. Why couldn't I think of anything more to say? I had always been graceful in both movement and conversation, but now I couldn't stop stuttering over my words and tried unsuccessfully to come up with something clever to say.

"But of course you will have your pick of the finest mounts in my—I mean, our kingdom. My father's stables breed excellent horses. We're known for them."

"I am honored." Damien could give me anything he liked and I would be ecstatic merely because it came from him, but I knew no other horse would ever replace Naomi in my affections.

When we reached the stables I called out to Theo to attend to Naomi and prepare her for riding. Damien then led me back to where his Cosan stood comfortably in one of our finest stalls, reserved for only the most esteemed and honored guests' animals.

"What did I tell you?" Damien smirked when my jaw dropped at the impressive size and figure of the black stallion in front of me.

"He's incredible," I whispered in awe. "I've never seen such a majestic, imposing animal in my life," I conceded.

"I thought you might be impressed." Damien stood and stroked the horse's gleaming neck and I watched as the muscles rippled through his massive torso. "He is the finest horse in my father's kingdom."

In an attempt to distract myself from his close proximity and the privacy of our current position, I reached up to stroke the horse's mane. After a moment Damien's hand found mine and he grasped it softly yet firmly and came closer to me. I slowly looked up at him in a sort of terrified anticipation. I felt completely out of my element here. He saw my feelings in a glance and laughed softly.

"You know, Aurora, I've been feeling quite strange about something."

"You have?" I asked.

"Yes, well, I realize our first kiss makes a great story for the grandchildren, but I'd prefer that you remember it," he teased.

"Oh, yes, that is rather strange, isn't it?" I shifted my weight nervously.

"Shall we remedy that? Or at least try to start over?"

I looked up in question. He stuck out his hand to grasp mine and then bowed over it gallantly. "Prince Damien at your service, ma'am. It is so very nice to meet you."

"Oh, yes, indeed," I played along. "I am Princess Aurora Claire, you may call me Claire," I responded with a curtsey.

"Excellent," he enthused. "Now, seeing as how we got that out of the way, when shall we get married?"

I giggled and pretended to swoon. "Why, whenever you wish it, Your Highness."

"Well, it can't come too soon for me. And in any case we should probably get this over with—" And with no further warning, he swept me into his arms and kissed me. I always thought my mind would go numbingly blank during my first real kiss. But instead it filled with a whirl of questions and observations. Was this kiss magical? Did I feel any magic? I felt a little dizzy. His lips felt warm, but his face was slightly stubbly. Was that normal? Was I falling in love? Was he? Should I already be in love? I had only known the man a couple of days. It was all very confusing.

He pulled back just enough to allow a hint of space between us and I opened my eyes to see his face above mine.

"Shall we take our ride now?" Damien asked with a smile.

"Um, yes. Yes, let's," I stammered. "Theo! Is Naomi ready?" I called out, while starting to walk out of the stable. Damien squeezed my hand before he released me completely and turned his attention to Cosan. Once on our horses we galloped away from the stables, enjoying the wind in our hair. I showed Damien around many of my favorite places from my childhood. I also showed him many of the shortcuts and back gates around the palace. By the time we returned to the stables it was nearly sundown. We parted to dress for supper, but joined again shortly in the dining hall where we took our now customary seats next to each other. That night I lay in bed with a smile on my face. It faded eventually as the now familiar dread and fear crept in. I groaned and flung my arm over my eyes. I don't remember falling asleep, but I must have because eventually I dreamed.

The glimmer that came from the small blade fascinated and terrified me all at once. I had swiped it from one of the servants. My gracefulness is good for more than dancing, I thought with excitement. He hadn't even seen me as I deftly fished it from his side belt before disappearing behind a tapestry. At ten, I had yet to have anything so sharp or danger- ous near my person. I wasn't even allowed to learn embroidery, although I was assured I would have excelled in that skill. I knew my parents were trying to protect me. They didn't want me to be afraid. But withholding them had only made them more fascinating. I again felt the cool, heavy weight that came from the knife before refolding it and placing it care- fully in the pocket of my overskirt.

Careful not to be seen, I snuck out into the garden. Once there I ran quickly to my willow tree. Stepping reverently over the stones, I reached the trunk and felt the rough bark beneath my hands. The deep grooves would present a bit of a problem. Not to be discouraged, I pulled out the knife and started carving. Deep, wide letters. Each took long, painstak- ing effort. At one point I lost control and the sharp tip grazed my left thumb, placed against the trunk for support. I gasped as a tiny bead of my blood appeared. I stared in fascination. I thought I might be fright- ened. I thought that maybe I should be. But instead, I could only stare at it and wonder what all the fuss was about. What made that evil fairy so set on causing that drop of blood anyhow?

I awoke early the next morning. I felt surprised, although I wasn't sure why. I lay there under my blankets for a while thinking and let- ting myself wake fully as I stretched luxuriously. As I did I realized the origin of my surprised feelings and I immediately tensed.

I had slept well. I actually felt rested. It must not have been a very long time before I succumbed to sleep last night. My fears seemed a little less potent now that I looked back on the night before. I felt myself relax and smile a little. Could it be I was finally getting used to all this? Was I free of my fear of the dark and dreams and sleeping in general? It would take several nights of peaceful slum- ber to be certain, but this was a very good sign and I sat up in bed with a grin. I wandered over to my window seat and glanced out the window. The sun was slowly making its way above the horizon and into its rightful place in the sky. There is something innately hopeful about a sunrise. I felt my spirits rise further with sun and I pranced over to my dressing table. My mood was suddenly dashed when I saw another freckle on my nose and the slight puffiness around my eyes. What was happening? I hoped and prayed this was only some strange phase I was going through. Angeline and her helpers came in just then so I turned to greet them.

"Good morning, ladies," I smiled. "I trust you slept well."

"Yes, ma'am," Angeline answered while Corrine and Annette nodded and smiled in agreement.

"I fear I've produced another freckle," I pointed a finger at my nose.

"Nothing a few puffs of beauty powder can't cure," Angeline assured me.

I leaned my elbows on the table and placed my chin in my hands.

"I suppose so," I mumbled.

The ladies got to work beautifying me and dressing me and sprinkling me with sweet smelling oils. I was getting used to the tangles in my hair and I only teared up once while they fashioned it into a glorious design of interwoven braids and curls. As I stood in front of the full-length mirror I nodded once in satisfaction. The warm blush tone of my satin gown made my cheeks glow and my eyes sparkle.

"Thank you," I said sweetly.

"Of course, Your Highness," they said admiringly. I turned and fairly skipped out of the room. On my way to the dining hall for breakfast I collided with someone coming around a corner.

I struggled to maintain my balance and looked up.

"Sir James," I said. "I'm sorry."

"It's my fault, Your Highness," he responded automatically. "Are you alright?"

"Yes, I'm fine, thank you. And you?"

"Oh, yes. Quite. Fine, that is."

"Good, good." Then I furrowed my brow. "I'm actually a little worried," I admitted. He looked at me in question.

"I hate to sound silly, but did you mess up my hair?"

His face was blank for a moment.

"Um, no? I don't think so."

"Well that's a relief," I sighed and turned to keep walking. When he didn't immediately join me I gave my eyes a mini roll and beckoned to him, somewhat exaggeratedly. I waited to continue until he walked beside me.

"You see, my hair never used to get mussed. I never bumped into anyone for that matter," I paused for a moment, thinking that over. Sir James looked entirely confused. "Well anyhow, the fact of the matter is that I think my ladies in waiting did quite a good job with it today. My hair, I mean. Don't you?" I angled my head around for his inspection.

"Um, yes," was his hesitant response. This man was notoriously hard to please.

"Mmm, well, I'm famished. I hope we have strawberries this morning. They're my favorite." We arrived at the entrance to the dining hall.

"Here we are," I announced unnecessarily. He nodded and left me to take his seat. Damien entered a few moments later and took my hands in his.

"Darling," he enthused with an exaggerated appraisal of my person. "You look scrumptious this morning." I blushed and did a happy little shrug.

"Do we have strawberries?" I asked Claudine, one of our kitchen maids, as she passed.

"Yes, we do, Your Highness," she smiled at me and curtsied.

"Lovely!" I clapped my hands and followed Damien to our chairs. My parents then entered, hand in hand, and we all rose until they took their seats. Breakfast passed uneventfully for the most part. I enjoyed my strawberries and shortcake. I also enjoyed Damien's hand as it seemingly accidentally brushed against mine once under the table.

After breakfast we discovered that we rode well together and I showed him more of my favorite places from my childhood until deciding to stop at a clearing filled with wild roses, near a little stone wall and a crumbling, long since abandoned hut. After dismounting, Damien spread out a blanket for the both of us to sit on while admiring the nature around us.

"Here you are, sweet," Damien said as he helped me sit down. I bent my knees and modestly tucked my ankles under my skirt.

"Isn't it the loveliest day?" I shut my eyes and felt the sunshine warm my face.

"Indeed," Damien agreed. We were both quiet for a little while after that. I found I didn't have anything to say and Damien seemed content to sit in silence. That silence was broken when we heard hooves pounding nearby. We both turned to see Sir James riding by.

"James!" Damien called out to him. Sir James slowed his horse and turned back to trot over to us on the blanket.

"Your Highness?" James asked.

"Get off that horse," Damien commanded with an easy smile. "What can you possibly have to do on this most perfect day that you must go gallivanting about as though the devil were at your heels? Sit here a while and entertain us."

I thought Sir James looked annoyed, but he dismounted obediently and stalked over to us. After a moment's hesitation he sat on a rock a few feet away. He seemed a very odd choice for an entertainer.

"What would you have me do?" he asked, grumbled rather.

"Well, how should I know?" Damien responded, somewhat exasperated. "But think of something. You're as dull and solemn as that stone wall behind you."

I took pity on Sir James.

"Tell me about Damien," I said. "What was he like as a child?"

Sir James opened his mouth, but Damien spoke before he could.

"We hardly grew up together, Aurora," he informed me. "Besides, I was exactly as you see me now. Handsome, sweet, and devilishly charming. All my governesses adored me." He laughed and I caught Sir James rolling his eyes.

"And where did you grow up, Sir James?" I asked. Again, Damien interrupted before James could speak.

"For goodness' sake, call him James, darling. That formality sounds ridiculous," he drawled. I looked to Sir James for approval. He nodded. He looked bored and uncomfortable. But then again he almost always looked like that.

"Well then, James," I said. "Where were you off to in such a hurry before we so rudely stopped you?"

"I was just riding," he answered. "Damien was right. I don't have anything to do today. As usual."

"How dreary you are lately," Damien scolded. "How can you be so dull in the face of such cheerful beauty?" He motioned at me and kissed my hand. I squirmed where normally such a compliment and gesture would make me smile. Sir James—James certainly knew how to dampen a mood.

"I'm sorry," James apologized. "I'm just eager to be back to my normal duties. At *home*." Damien ignored his obvious emphasis on the word and turned back to me.

"Well, I'm in no hurry to go anywhere. Darling, be an angel and smooth your fingers over my forehead, will you? I'm getting a headache." He laid back and closed his eyes.

Hesitantly at first, I did as he asked. I marveled for what must be the hundredth time at his beauty as I softly brushed back his hair. It was soon apparent that he had fallen asleep. His breathing deepened and he began to snore very softly. I folded my hands in my lap while James and I both pretended we didn't feel as awkward as we did. Damien snorted once and then rolled onto his side. I bit back a giggle and caught James's eye. My smile spread and I covered my mouth to muffle any emerging sounds of laughter. He fought it, but eventually he gave in and smiled himself.

"Can I show you something?" I whispered.

He looked surprised but nodded. I stood and motioned for him to follow me. We walked around the old stone wall and down a few paces where the ivy grew thick and a drooping willow tree swayed gently next to a tiny pond. I pulled back a few branches and held them so James could follow me. Near the trunk, I knelt down, careful not to get dirt on my gown.

"Here," I pointed at several large, flat stones placed strategically on the ground.

"What are they?" James asked.

"They're tomb stones," I explained.

James looked confused, and quite frankly, a little disturbed.

"Oh, they're just for animals," I rushed to explain. James didn't look as though that made it any better. "Is that strange?" I flustered. "When I was little, if I found a dead bird or squirrel or lizard, I would take them here and have a sort of burial service for them."

He nodded in tentative understanding.

"I thought that when I went to sleep and finally woke up again all the animals I had ever seen on these grounds would be dead and gone. I hated to think that the birds I loved to hear singing near my window, or the lizards I tried to catch, and squirrels I would feed when I snuck into the orchards would all be gone. So whenever I found one that had already died, I would bring it here so at least I could have a place to mourn them when I woke up." I looked up at James. "Is that so very odd?" I laughed, embarrassed. I supposed saying it out loud *did* make it sound silly. Bizarre, even.

At his silence I continued, "Well, *you* try going through life knowing you're going to sleep for a hundred years when you turn sixteen and see if you don't turn out a little strange yourself."

James knelt beside me and examined a stone. "I actually don't think it sounds strange at all," he said simply. "My sister and I buried dead animals that we found too. I'm sure most children do. I think it is part of coming to terms with death and its inevitability. In your case, it was just a little more meaningful."

"Oh, well, thank you, I guess," I said and then laughed at myself again. "And this," I said pointing to the tree trunk, "is where I carved my initials after I stole a pocket knife from one of the footmen."

James laughed appreciatively and touched the crude carving.

"P. A. C. + M. T. L.?" he asked, squinting.

"Princess Aurora Claire and *My True Love*," I informed him, smiling at my silliness.

"How old were you?"

"Around ten, I think."

"Very nice."

"Thank you," I laughed. "This was rather adventurous of me, you know," I informed him. "I wasn't allowed to play with anything remotely sharp, due to my curse. My parents thought sharp objects would remind me of a spindle and frighten me, which they did, but I think that's why I was drawn to them. I wanted to conquer my fear of them or show my command over them or something," I waved my hand at my foolishness. "So I was always pocketing knives, and sewing needles, and whatever else I found. I made the servants crazy with my antics."

"I didn't know I was in the presence of a renowned knife thief," James said with mock respect.

I nearly gaped at him with my mouth hanging open. Luckily my tact came through and I simply responded in kind.

"Yes, well." I nodded proudly. "I was quite stealthy for my age."

"So I gather," was his response.

We both fell silent after that. I realized that we should probably get back to Damien before he awoke and found the two of us sitting within the intimate enclosure of a willow tree. This time James held back the branches for me as I passed through and I nodded my thanks.

"I'm sorry you find our palace so distasteful," I said as we walked the short distance to where Damien still lay on the ground.

"Oh, I don't," James shook his head. "It's not that. I'm simply eager to return home. It's been a very long time." I thought he might say more, but his face closed off again and I realized that I would have to be content with that answer.

Damien awoke when I sat down next to him.

"Oh, sorry, darling, I must have dozed off."

"Don't apologize," I smiled graciously. "James and I had a nice chat."

"Your hands must have the healing magic in them." He took one of the members he was describing and kissed it. "My headache seems to have vanished."

43

"I'm so glad." He helped me stand and we all walked back to our horses.

"I apologize if my request brings that headache back, Your Highness," James started, "but I would like to know when you're planning on returning to your kingdom. Merely so that I may begin making arrangements."

Damien waved his hand as though batting at an irritating fly.

"I am still working out all the details with Claire's father and his advisors. There are still marriage agreements and official alliance documents to be drafted. Once everything is settled, Claire and I shall send for my father to attend our wedding here. And once *that* is finished, we shall travel to our kingdom on our wedding tour."

This was mostly all news to me. I listened with interest.

"But now that you are here and have the protection of King Roland, I will no longer be needed. I could return home alone. You must have no further use for me." James was insistent.

"Nonsense, you shall remain here until we all travel back to Gaël together. There's no rush, is there?" This was phrased as more of a statement than a question.

James bowed curtly and mounted his horse. We followed suit and began riding back to the palace stables. The tension in the air was uncomfortable although Damien seemed unaffected. I couldn't understand why James must stay here when truly he wasn't needed. My father had an adequate army at his disposal and it would be at least a few months before wedding preparations would be finished and before the actual ceremony could take place. James already seemed strained by his lack of purpose and want for anything useful to do.

CHAPTER SIX

*A*fter leaving the stables I took a small luncheon in my quarters. I daydreamed about possible wedding gown designs while I nibbled on cold meats and cucumbers. That, of course, led to fantasies of the day itself and I soon became wrapped up in imagining myself waltzing down a long aisle with my handsome prince awaiting me at the end.

I jumped, startled out of my reverie, when Angeline nearly tumbled into the room in her haste. I hopped up and took her hands in my own while she steadied her breath.

"What is it, Ange?"

She gulped in a few more breaths and then led me over to my window seat. We both sat.

"Your Highness," she began, "Something's happened."

"What?" I pressed. "What's happened?" I felt a sinking feeling deep in my stomach. Had something happened to Damien?

"It's Cedric," she explained.

I looked back at her blankly.

"Who?"

"He's a lower footman for His Majesty's counselor Lord Douglas."

"What's become of him?"

She hesitated. She looked like she dreaded sharing whatever information she had. "He's . . . asleep."

"What do you mean? He fell asleep while he was supposed to be working? And now he'll be punished? Really, Ange, you aren't making much sense. What has this got to do with me? And why are you shaking like that?"

"No, you don't understand, Your Highness," she hesitated yet again. She bit her lip and quietly said, "They can't wake him up."

My mind refused to register what she had said for a few moments. I blinked stupidly while my surroundings suddenly became large and stifling. The information came with full force then and hit me like a blast of icy wind. My stomach dropped and I felt an intense pain starting to build behind my eyes.

"What—what are you saying?" I stammered. "He's asleep? Well, fetch a doctor. Wake him up. Someone just needs to wake him up." I felt my body go rigid and my voice sounded harsh and tight.

Angeline shook her head slowly and tried to draw my hands into her own, but I wouldn't budge.

"They've tried everything. Even the royal physician has examined him and can't manage to rouse him from sleep. He says . . ." her voice faltered momentarily. She cleared her throat and began again. "The physician says that his body is healthy, nothing seems to be wrong with him. He hasn't even lapsed into a coma or stupor. He's just sleeping. It appears to be exactly like—"

I stood and began pacing.

"Alright, he was tired. So tired from working that he fell into a deep slumber. I've always felt that Lord Douglas works too hard. I'm sure the effect from his work ethic trickles all the way down. The poor man was probably exhausted. I'll speak to Father about it. We mustn't work people so hard. There's no excuse for that."

Angeline rose and reached out to me, stopping me in my tracks and halting my rambling. My lower lip trembled and I wordlessly clenched and unclenched my fists. I did my best to hold it in, but my face crumbled and the rest of me followed. Angeline caught me in her arms and stroked my hair while I choked on hot, furious tears.

"What can this mean?" I moaned between jagged breaths.

"You're parents wish to see you in the east wing council room," she said quietly.

My feet practically flew through the hallways and corridors. I burst through the wide doors into the council room and saw my mother's dejected form hunched over as she rested her head in her hands. My father stood behind her with a hand on her shoulders.

"Mother? Father?" I asked hesitantly.

They both turned quickly and rushed to meet me. We embraced and they whispered words of comfort, but I couldn't hear them. I couldn't hear anything except the rushing of blood in my ears and my own heartbeat, which sounded like an enormous clock ticking ominously.

"Why is this happening?" I asked numbly. My tears started to come afresh.

"We don't know, Claire, my love," my father answered sorrowfully. "But I promise you that we'll get to the bottom of this."

I nodded at him, but I didn't feel reassured. I then noticed that the room was nearly full. Every advisor, counselor, and companion of my father was present. At his request they all took their place along the long table in the center of the room.

"I thought it important that the princess be present for this discussion," my father said, guiding me to a seat at his left while my mother took her place at his right.

"Where is Prince Damien?" he asked Sir Helmsly, who sat several seats away.

My head snapped up. Of course. Where was he?

"He will be here shortly, your majesty," Sir Helmsly answered. "He has been summoned."

At that very moment Damien opened the doors and walked swiftly into the room. He was followed by James.

"What is the meaning of this?" Damien demanded. "I've been informed that someone fell asleep and that my presence was requested?" He sounded intensely annoyed. As though he couldn't fathom why he was needed because of some inconsequential matter. My stomach clenched when I realized he hadn't made the connection. What would his reaction be? Would he want to call off our engagement?

"Yes, Your Highness," my father's first counselor, Lord Shepherd, said, rising to show Damien and James to their places.

"You see, Prince Damien," my father began, "It seems that one of the footmen here at the castle has fallen into a sort of coma. Only, it's not a coma." He hesitated.

"He's back under the spell," I burst out. I was sick of people tip-toeing around the issue.

"What?" Damien asked, alarmed.

James leaned forward in his chair. "How is that possible?" he asked.

My father motioned to Silvien, the royal physician, to speak.

"Well, I've examined the lad and all of his, um, symptoms are or rather his present condition is exactly consistent with what we know of the spell's sleep."

"How can you know that?" Damien asked roughly. "Weren't you all sleeping? How do you know what it looked like?"

"Begging your pardon, Your Highness, but the princess fell asleep several hours before anyone else did," Silvien defended himself.

Sir Chester piped up. "You see, once the princess—er . . . fell asleep, there was a tremendous flash and the king rushed to the tower only to find his beloved daughter unconscious on the stone floor."

"Must you be so callous about it?" my father asked angrily. Sir Chester went off into a fluster of apologies.

"It's alright," I said, shutting my eyes and mentally willing every-one to stop making a fuss over it.

"Anyway," now it was Lord Tristan who braved the telling of the tale. "The princess was examined carefully by Silvien who concluded that she was simply asleep just as the curse had detailed. We then placed Princess Aurora Claire in the tower that had been prepared for her and His and Her Majesties the king and queen retired to their rooms in distress."

My mother now took up the narrative.

"We were so distraught. I don't remember what happened then, but the next thing I knew, we awoke to find Claire running into our room. It was the happiest moment of my life." She choked on a small sob and couldn't continue. I bit my lip and cursed my eyes for beginning to water yet again.

After several other personal accounts of what had happened after I had fallen asleep it seemed to be the general consensus that everyone had gone to sleep at more or less the exact same time. I had a sudden inspiration.

"It must have been Bernadette," I blurted.

"What was that?" my father turned to me.

"Who is Bernadette?" Damien demanded.

"Bernadette. She was the last fairy to give me a gift. She is the one who amended Zora's gift from death to a hundred years of sleep." I turned to my father. "She must have seen you and mother suffering and decided to place the entire castle under the spell. What else would have caused the sleep to spread to everyone within the walls of the palace?" Everyone looked at me. "The plan was to keep me locked in my tower, right? I was to be under careful watch and care with strict instructions to each subsequent generation until my hundred years were up and my rescuer appeared. How else do you explain the change of events?"

"She makes a good point, your majesty," Lord Shepherd said. "Who else would have had the power and the motivation to take pity on yours and the queen's situation?"

"Very true," my father agreed.

Just then a footman appeared at the door and cleared his throat.

"Yes, what is it?" Lord Shepherd asked distractedly.

"Begging your majesty's pardon, but something's come up," he responded.

My father sat up straighter and acknowledged the young man.

"There—there's been another . . . case."

"Another case?" my father asked.

"Another person has fallen asleep."

CHAPTER SEVEN

*T*he meeting was adjourned so that Silvien could rush to examine the sleeping person. This time it was a woman. Her name was Madeleine and she worked in the kitchens as an apprentice pastry cook. My father and his advisors huddled together near her sleeping form to discuss possible courses of action. I heard bits and pieces. Find a cure . . . Horrible business with magic . . . Fairy Council.

Of course! I rushed to my father.

"We must ask the Council of Seven what is happening," I urged.

"Yes, Claire," he tucked my hand in the crook of his arm. "I'm afraid you're right."

Approaching the Council of Seven was not an easy task. Fairies were notoriously temperamental as evidenced by my horrible fairy-given curse. Damien, who was standing nearby, came forward.

"Sir James and I will go to the Fairy Council," he announced. "I insist upon it. You must all stay here and attend to the crisis. We will travel there and find out what is happening here."

I turned to him gratefully and smiled through my tears. He flashed a smile back at me and winked. My father began thanking him profusely.

It was soon settled that Damien and James would leave the following morning.

I spent a few hours in my room after leaving Madeleine's chambers. These two people who had fallen back under the spell were not exactly in the forefront of important people at the castle. Maybe the sleep would only claim these two. If it kept going maybe it would start with those of little or no nobility. Perhaps there was some lingering effect from the fairy magic. Perhaps these two had weaker constitutions and they couldn't withstand the . . . Thoughts trailed off and I shook my head. There shouldn't have been any lingering magic. The curse was over. Fulfilled. There was no comprehensible reason that I could see for such a relapse. I stared out my window and watched the sun slowly setting. It seemed so long ago that I watched it rise, full of hope and promise. Was it really just this morning? I feared the darkness that would soon cover the castle. I had no reason to think that I was safe from this relapse. My thoughts were interrupted by a knock on my door.

"Who is it?" I asked.

"Sir Hector," a voice replied. Sir Hector was my father's personal valet. What was he doing here? I ran to the door and opened it. Sir Hector stood there with worry etched so deeply in his face I barely recognized him in the candlelight.

"What is it?" I begged, trying to subdue the horrible sinking feeling in my stomach.

"You're needed in your parents' chambers," he motioned for me to follow him, but he avoided my gaze.

"Why?" I didn't budge. "What's happened?"

Sir Hector sighed.

"Your father, His Majesty, has fallen asleep. They cannot wake him."

"No!" I gasped and rushed past him to sprint though the corridors. I heard Sir Hector behind me as we made our way swiftly to the king's chambers.

My mother stood near the bed, holding a handkerchief to her face. I hurried to her side and saw my father lying serenely on sheets of creamy silk. I stroked a hand over his forehead as a tear made its way down my nose until it fell onto my father's robe. I brushed it away and turned to throw my arms around my mother who cried with me.

"I'm so sorry, Mother," I sobbed in her ear.

"My darling," she soothed, "it isn't your fault. Don't think such things." She pulled away and wiped my face with her handkerchief. "Don't worry, all will be well. Tomorrow your handsome prince will leave to ask the Council of Seven for the meaning of this. He'll get to the bottom of it. Don't you fret."

Her words were soothing, but I couldn't shake the feeling of guilt. I nodded once and gave her a hug. Angeline appeared at my side to escort me to my room. Supper would be taken privately tonight as the queen and I were indisposed and Prince Damien and Sir James would need a good night's sleep for their early departure tomorrow. I embraced Angeline before she left me with my supper tray. I picked uninterestedly at the food until giving up and returning to my window seat. I didn't want to be anywhere near my bed right now. I pressed my forehead against the cool glass. The usual calming effect didn't come and I stared hopelessly out at the darkness. If my father were susceptible, who would be next? And what was the time frame? There were thousands of people within the castle grounds. If we continued at a rate of three or four per day how long did we have? A journey to the Fairy Council would take approximately three days of hard riding. Damien and James would be gone at least a week. If we continued on at a similar pace here, they should return with ample time to save everyone again. But what if it sped up? What if tomorrow people began to fall by the hundreds? Would Damien and James have time? Could they save us again? I stared in resentment at my bed and again out at the darkness. I would never be able to sit here idly while waiting for their return. I would go mad with worry. It was different waiting to fall asleep the first time. This was never part of the plan. I closed my eyes and tried to quiet my restless thoughts.

There was something strange in the way I felt the morning I turned fifteen. I think everyone would agree that this was to be expected. It was my last real birthday before my, well, my long break from normal birthdays. But I didn't think I felt fear, as I supposed I might. I felt a sort of heroism. I felt like I finally understood what my tutors, my parents, my governances and handmaids had always told me. There was beauty in my future. Not really in its poetry or romance, although a part of me had that idea thoroughly ingrained as well, but in its self-sacrifice. By taking the punishment, I spared an entire kingdom pain and suffering. I alone could save them from an age-old feud—though I still didn't quite understand what it was. Zora hated my parents. She was punishing them through me. But if I made the best of the situation—if I didn't let my parents see my fear, I could make it easier on them. I could take away just a little bit of Zora's victory. So I walked proudly into my birthday celebration and smiled radiantly at the faces I saw tentatively smiling back at me. I saw my parent's trepidation. Naturally, they worried how this birthday would affect me. I could see how it affected them. I held my head up high and took my place at the table.

It was well past midnight when my body jerked and I awakened with a jolt and the sensation of falling off a step. I realized I had drifted off to a restless sleep. Something in that short amount of sleep had given me clarity. I rushed to the window and threw it open, forcing deep, cool breaths in and out of my constricted chest. A calm finally settled over me. After days of uneasily feeling out how my life was supposed to continue with the lack of direction previously incessantly imposed on me, I knew what I had to do.

Damien and Sir James were going to have an unexpected traveling companion. There was no way I would be able to sit here and wait for their return. And really, it was my place to go. My responsibility. It always had been.

With father now asleep I didn't have to fear his disapproval and his forbidding me from going. I stretched my stiff limbs, walked purposefully across the room, and unlatched my door. The way to my parent's chambers seemed much shorter this time as I walked soundlessly over the cool stone floor. I pushed open the heavy door and saw my mother dozing fitfully on a chair near the fireplace to the right of the bed where my father still lay. Careful not to make any loud noises, I tiptoed to my mother's side and gently nudged her shoulder until her head snapped up and she looked around wildly.

"I'm sorry to wake you, Mother," I apologized, taking her hands in my own.

Her bloodshot eyes slowly gained recognition as she looked at me.

"Can't you sleep, dear one?" she asked and motioned for me to cuddle next to her on her chair. At that moment I wanted nothing more than to sit in her arms and forget the world that had come crashing down around me, but I forced myself to stick to my plan.

"Mother, I have something to ask you. But I must warn you. I will not be persuaded to change my mind. I'm asking you because I love you and respect you, but I intend to follow through despite your answer." I spoke carefully yet with gentle finality. Mother looked at me in surprise. She had never heard me speak this way. *I* had never heard *myself* speak this way.

"I'm going with Damien and Sir James," I began. She sat up and started to protest, but I held out my hand. "Please, Mother, you must understand. I cannot sit here and wait for them to return. I've spent my whole life waiting. I cannot do it anymore. I refuse to do it anymore. My mind is made up. I must go."

"Have you considered the dangers of an unaccompanied journey like that?" Mother asked.

"I'll be with Damien and Sir James. We'll disguise ourselves as nobility. No one will know we're royal."

"You're naïve to think that your identities will remain a secret," she argued.

"No one even knows about my story. People have forgotten all about us," I countered. "Besides, Sir James and Damien will give me all the protection I need." I felt confident in that.

"Have you even asked them about this scheme of yours? How do you know they'll agree to take you along? The risk they take to do this for us will grow exponentially if you accompany them."

I hadn't thought of them not agreeing with my plan. I was sure I could make Damien see my point of view. James might be another story. But I knew I could be helpful.

"I will question them tomorrow before they leave," I told Mother. "I'm sure I can convince them to see it my way."

I saw the sadness and resignation in my mother's eyes and I knew I had won. She was too weary to argue further. She kissed my forehead and hugged me tightly.

"I wish you well on your journey, my sweet," she whispered in my ear. "Be careful and be brave. Come back to me."

"I will," I whispered back. I kissed her cheek and left without looking back. Although it was what fueled me and gave me my strength and my purpose, I didn't trust myself to look once more at what I was leaving behind.

CHAPTER EIGHT

*O*nce I got back to my room, I rang for Angeline who groggily entered a few minutes later.

"What is it, Your Highness?" she asked, covering a yawn.

"I'm going with Prince Damien," I announced boldly. "I need you to help me pack."

Angeline stared at me blankly.

"Don't just stand there," I urged. "We have much to do before dawn." I reached for a small traveling case and began dragging my simplest and plainest gowns from my wardrobe. Angeline snapped out of her stupor and joined me.

"How is this possible?" she asked. "Did you ask your mother?"

"Yes, I did."

"And?"

"She's not happy, but I told her there's no stopping me and she believed me."

"Alright then," she said, a little impressed, I think. She helped me choose the gowns that fastened in the front and taught me how to tie them. These were the gowns that would draw the least attention and she showed me how to pack them saving the most room and causing the least amount of wrinkles. While we packed we talked about my impending journey.

"Is Prince Damien happy with your decision?"

"I haven't told him yet."

"Well, when are you planning on doing that?"

"I thought I'd tell them in the stables when they go to leave. Sort of surprise attack them so they don't have much time to think about it."

"Might work." Angeline sounded dubious.

"I have a few stirring arguments."

"Which are?"

"Um, that I can more persuasively plead our case to the Council of Seven due to my personal experience with them. I have also met and have an understanding of Bernadette, which should help."

"You met her when you were three months old."

"That's a trivial detail."

We finished filling my case with the necessities and Angeline helped me dress in a dark green gown. It was made of thick, muslin which was of quality but certainly not glamorous. My cloak was gray and drab. I examined myself in the mirror and frowned slightly. I looked tired and my eyes were still a bit puffy from crying. The dreary colors I wore did little to brighten my face. I couldn't wait to get my gifts back.

"You look perfect," Angeline assured me. "Not too royal."

"I was more worried about my looking 'not too gorgeous' at the moment," I said with a wry smile. "My number one argument, after all, is a pretty smile and an effectively timed pout."

Angeline grinned and shook her head.

"You've never needed to know this, but if you're looking pale you can pinch your cheeks like this," she demonstrated for me. I saw a pleasing tone of pink return to my cheeks.

"Now, lick your lips and smack them like this." Another demonstration. I did so and a delicate rosiness puckered up my pout just beautifully.

"Thanks for the tips," I wiggled my eyebrows at her and she laughed.

"Well," she said, holding me at arm's length. "You're ready."

"I believe I am," I said, nervousness suddenly clutching my stomach.

"I'll walk with you to the stables," she offered.

"That's not necessary," I told her.

"Of course it is," she argued. "I'll go grab you a roll and some fruit from the kitchen for your breakfast." As if on cue, my stomach grumbled and I smiled at her gratefully.

We walked quietly toward the kitchen and I waited outside the main doors while she darted in. She came back out a few moments later carrying a wrapped loaf of bread and a small sack of apples.

"It's not much, certainly not what you're used to, but it will tide you over," she whispered as we continued on to an unguarded door to the west courtyard. Once there we snuck across, narrowly avoiding being seen by a wandering guard. We ran to the stables, surefooted in the darkness. Pressed against the side of the large stone structure, we caught our breath. I clutched my bundle of food and my traveling case to my chest. There was no going back now. I hugged Angeline and thanked her again.

"It was nothing, Your Highness," she insisted. "Be safe and best of luck to you all." She spoke for everyone. Everyone was counting on the outcome of this journey.

"I won't let you down," I promised as much to myself as to her.

I watched her run back toward the castle and duck into a side door, avoiding Alvin and Theo, who were sleeping on two cots near the entrance. I slipped into Naomi's stall and soothed her flustered movements with a pat on the nose and a comforting whisper in her ear. I then got to work practicing saddling and unsaddling Naomi. I had seen Alvin and Theo do it countless times. I couldn't believe how heavy it was. But with the mounting block's help I finally got the hang of it. I just didn't know what I'd do once we were on our way without the help of the stable. I slowly sank down to sit on the soft hay on the floor of the stall and waited for dawn.

I heard voices and my head jerked up. I had dozed off, but it couldn't have been for very long. The dim gray of the coming dawn was just beginning to show when I glanced out the window above Naomi's stall.

"Come now, James, this errand will take a week at most and then we'll continue on schedule." That was Damien's voice.

"I hope so," James answered back. The voices moved past my location and continued on toward the guest stalls at the end. I carefully exited my hiding place just as they entered Cosan's stall. I followed quietly and at the entrance I nervously cleared my throat.

James whirled around in surprise. The surprise grew to bewilderment when he realized I was the intruder. Damien looked shocked as well, though he recovered quickly.

"Darling," he came over to me to take my hands in his. "Did you come to see us off? How sweet of you." He kissed me on my cheek.

"No, actually," I said. I steeled myself for any and all possible reactions to what I was about to say. "I'm coming with you."

James looked confused and Damien started laughing.

"This is hardly the time for joking," he chuckled.

"I'm quite serious, I assure you." My tone was firm.

"I apologize, Your Highness, but that isn't even an option," James frowned and his tone was curt, annoyed.

"Why not?" I demanded.

"Well, you would slow us down for one thing," James answered. "Also, it's much too dangerous for you to travel with so small a party."

"But I have the two of you strong and capable men for protection," I reasoned with a coy smile. Damien grinned. He knew what I was doing. James seemed to know too, but his reaction was to look cross. Damien smacked him on the arm.

"Come, James, are you not as confident in your abilities in security as I thought you were? Surely you can handle protecting us all." His voice was teasing and self-deprecating and I found myself charmed by him yet again.

James grumbled.

"And I wouldn't slow you down," I insisted, moving the topic along and keeping my eyes on Damien who seemed to be weakening in his resolve. "You've both seen me ride. I'm very good. I'm strong too. And hardy." I mean, that was a bit of an exaggeration, but I kept my chin up, daring either of them to call my bluff. Which James did.

"You?" James scoffed.

"How would you even know, anyway?" I whirled back toward him, irritated.

"You've never once left the castle grounds," he retorted quickly. "How would *you* know?"

Damien rolled his eyes at the both of us. I took a deep breath to calm myself.

"Look, I have personal experience with Bernadette and with this curse. Obviously. I can make a better case. Fairies are notoriously hard to deal with. The more we have on our side to work with the better." I presented my case with as much earnest zeal as I could muster.

"I can't argue with that, Aurora, but there remains one main problem," Damien said.

"Which is what?" I asked.

"I hate to sound callous, darling, but what if you were to . . . suc-cumb to—that is, what if you . . . fall asleep while we are away? How can we carry you around when you're like that?"

I had expected the question, the problem had entered my own mind during the night, but it still stung to hear it voiced aloud.

"I don't know if I can convince you, but somehow I know that I won't. I'm almost positive that I will be last. It's happening in reverse now, and in slow motion. Before—the first time—I fell and then nearly a full day later everyone else did. This time I will be last. I just know."

"There is still the issue of danger. You're a huge liability." James pressed.

"Alright, I'll grant you that," I conceded. "But there's just no way that I'm not going. This is my fault. This is my responsibility. And I've waited around my whole life for things to happen to me. I refuse to do that for a second longer. I need to go. I need to plead my case to the Council of Seven. I can't sit here and wait for more people to fall back under a curse that has hung over my head for my whole life. And so I'll say it again. I am going. With or without you, I am going."

My impassioned speech had the desired effect. I could have hugged myself for not allowing a tear to escape.

"If you're sure," Damien said.

"Very sure," I responded.

"James?" Damien turned to him.

"Fine," he almost growled in response.

"Good, now help her saddle her horse." He turned to me. "I assume you're packed and ready to go?"

"Of course," I nodded.

"We'll have to stop back at the kitchen to get additional food and supplies," James was still annoyed.

"I have enough for the day," I piped up.

James smiled humorlessly. "This isn't a day trip, Your Highness."

I swallowed my embarrassment and followed him back to Naomi's stall. He tied my case securely on Naomi's back. We all led our horses out of the stable and rode toward the kitchen. James entered and shortly came back with two medium-sized bundles. One he strapped on Naomi behind my case and the other he placed on his own horse.

"Ready," he announced. "Let's go."

We rode side by side with me between Damien and James. An open gate beckoned. My heart beat faster as we neared it and then burst through.

I was on my way.

CHAPTER NINE

The first day of our journey passed as a blur. We rode hard and long with two or three stops for food, relief, and to rest and water the horses. My eyes seemed to become numb under the constant barrage of scenery racing past me and my hands stung from blisters where I held the reigns. My backside ached and my legs felt limp and wobbly each time we dismounted. My skirts were long enough that I could ride astride my horse, rather than bother with a sidesaddle. That would have never worked with the pace these men kept. However, the fact that I hadn't slept more than half an hour the previous night was catching up to me. I struggled to hide my fatigue from Damien and James who both watched me closely. I kept finding myself plastering on a bright smile and saying "I'm fine," over and over to all their inquiries. I was not fine. By the time we finally stopped for the night and James set up our three tents, I stumbled into mine and promptly fell asleep. I didn't have time to worry and fear about the possibility of not waking up. Or the possibility of more of my friends and family falling asleep. I didn't even have the energy to dream, it seemed. I slept the sleep like the dead, although that's a horrible and, in my case, all too frighteningly appropriate way of putting it.

I woke with a start the next morning. Damien was calling my name from outside my tent.

"You know, you really can call me Claire," I reminded him, rubbing my eyes.

"Oh, but Aurora is so beautiful." he smiled. I was too tired to determine what I made of that so I just shrugged.

"We need to get going," he urged. "There's a stream nearby for you to wash up."

I smoothed down my unruly hair and stumbled out into the sunlight. I was still dressed in my green gown and I did my best to avoid eye contact with the two men. They had seen me once before when I had just woken up, but that was when my gifts were still happily working to make me look portrait-ready at any time of day.

It was early and the bright morning rays felt warm on my face as I splashed water on my face and drunk greedily. Feeling much more refreshed, I hurried back to our camp and saw that James was almost done packing up my tent and strapping it on the back of Naomi.

"Thank you," I told him. He nodded and handed me a roll of bread and a small satchel of nuts.

"Breakfast," he informed me. "Eat it while you ride. You slept in."

"Well, you could have woken me earlier," I grumbled under my breath. He was already mounting his horse and if he heard me, he didn't acknowledge it. I stuffed bread into my mouth, found a large rock to use as a block, and pulled myself up onto Naomi's saddle. The muscles in my legs revolted as I forced myself to get into riding position. I was in excruciating pain.

"Everything alright?" Damien asked. I gritted my teeth.

"Wonderful," I said.

"We need to get moving," James called.

"Well, I'm not stopping us," I snapped, then blushed and sighed apologetically. "Sorry, I'm ready. Let's go."

Thankfully, we stopped at a small village along the way for lunch. I stretched my aching legs and back before following Damien into a local inn for our meal. James tied up the horses and met us inside. The inn was humble but adequate. I was ravenous for a warm meal, and Damien and James both bit back laughter as they watched me devour my venison stew. I looked up expectantly.

"Sorry, darling," Damien chuckled. "I've never seen you so hungry."

"I didn't know a princess could eat like that," James said with what seemed like genuine surprise.

I scowled. "Let me eat in peace or I'll really make this journey unpleasant for you both. It's too late to send me back, you know." I reminded them, stuffing a bite of thick, dark bread drenched with stew into my mouth. Really, if I hadn't been so blasted hungry, exhausted, sore, and afraid, I would have been appalled by my unladylike behavior. I supposed my gifts of delicacy and grace were vanishing along with my beauty. It was a disturbing thought, but my stomach growled and I stuffed another bite in my mouth with a hopeless kind of shrug.

We finished the meal quickly and I bade the comfortable looking room a remorseful farewell. I tried to shake myself out of my dread of getting back on Naomi by reminding myself that I asked for this. And the alternative, waiting around at the castle for more people to relapse, was much worse than a few sore muscles. The day passed relatively quickly after that. By nightfall we were a little over half a day's ride from Faeria, the town where the most prominent fairies, namely those who made up the council, resided. James set up camp and I sat near the fire while Damien sang a minstrel song. It was sad and sweet and haunting.

"You sing beautifully," I complimented him. He smiled at me absently and tossed a twig into the fire.

"What about you? Do you sing?" he asked.

"Of course I can sing," I answered. "One of my fairy gifts is the gift of song, after all."

"Well then, let's hear something."

I readily cleared my throat and began a lovely tune about a maiden who got lost in a forest and then found a lonely fawn who led her back to her true love. After the first line I knew something was wrong. My notes wavered. My tone was weak. My vibrato was thin. I blushed and kept singing. It only got worse. I bravely sang an entire verse, but by the end I found I couldn't continue. I coughed once, trying to clear the lump in my throat.

"That was very nice," Damien struggled to sound sincere.

"Um, I don't understand," I faltered. "My voice usually sounds—" and then I realized the problem. My gift of song, like my gift of beauty, my gift of grace, and so many others, had started to disappear. I felt my eyes fill with tears and I excused myself quickly. I bumped into James on the way to my tent.

"Is my tent finished yet?" I asked, dashing the tears from my eyes.

"Yes," he looked concerned. "Are you alright?"

"You must have heard," I grimaced.

"What—you singing?"

"If you can call it that," I sniffed.

"Do you normally sound different?"

"Of course I do!" I exclaimed. "Do you think I would start singing if I knew I would sound so awful?"

"Well, I always think it's a little strange when people spontaneously start singing, no matter how well they sing."

I didn't know if he was trying to make me feel better or poke fun at me or simply make an observation.

"Perhaps it is, but at any rate, I used to have a beautiful voice. I used to have flawless skin. And I used to be incapable of tripping or bumping into anything. Ever." I huffed and stalked into my tent. As I closed the flap I saw James shake his head in confusion or disgust, I wasn't sure which. I also wasn't sure why I cared.

The next day we rode until mid afternoon, stopping only once for a brief snack of dried fruit and nuts and to water the horses. Thankfully, no one mentioned my embarrassing performance. We reached Faeria just after the Council of Seven convened for the day. We pounded on the tall, majestic doors in futility.

"Blasted fairies," Damien hissed under his breath. "Of all the rude, ridiculous . . ." he trailed off and I wasn't really listening anyway. I was too focused on my own disappointment.

"We'll go back to the village we passed a mile back," James proposed. Humans were not allowed to dwell, even temporarily, directly in Faeria. The village of Kern was the nearest human settlement. I sadly got back on Naomi and followed Damien and James over the well traveled dirt roads.

We reached the inn just before supper. The building was very small and humble, just like the village. No one seemed to care or even give us a second glance as we entered the inn to inquire about rooms for the night. Once settled in our respective quarters, we met back in the dining room for a meal of greasy pork and boiled potatoes. The mood at our table was low. We were all frustrated and tired and anxious for the following morning. I bid Damien and James goodnight before retiring to my room for a troubled sleep.

CHAPTER TEN

I woke up with a jolt the next morning. I groaned and rubbed my eyes. The bright sunshine streamed through the window next to the bed where I slept. Slowly I realized the monumental nature of this particular morning and nervousness flooded my empty stomach. I quickly dressed and walked into the dining room, hoping to see James and Damien nearby. The two men were seated at a table, eating apple turnovers and bacon. I joined them and tried to force down a few bites of my breakfast. James looked over at me as I pushed my food around. His head tilted to one side as he examined me closely. I finally met his gaze and widened my eyes in exasperation.

"What?" I exclaimed loudly, throwing up my hands. Several other patrons looked over at me in surprise at my outburst.

"Your appetite seems to have dwindled along with your manners," James smirked.

I shoved another bite of bacon in my mouth while I glared at him. James made a big show of trying not to laugh, but then sobered as Damien elbowed him sharply.

"How did you sleep?" Damien asked.

"Not very well," I admitted. "I was too nervous."

"Don't worry, darling," Damien said confidently. "We'll get to the bottom of this and be back home in no time."

"I hope so," I replied, taking a drink from a clay mug and dabbing delicately at my mouth with a rough cloth, still stinging from James's remark.

We reached the castle quickly and were admitted after abbreviating our reason for visiting to the guards outside of the large, sparkling structure. Bright lights twinkled and shimmered above and around us as we walked slowly into the great hall. It seemed as if the entire structure were constructed from finely cut crystal. Even the floor sparkled. I felt like I was inside a chandelier.

There was a long, ornately carved table at the head of the room that had an iridescent quality to it with wispy tufts and curves of finely spun silk and tulle hanging in delicate swirls behind the chairs, which sat seven exquisitely beautiful women. They stared down their narrow, perfectly formed noses at us as we approached. The fairy in the middle was clearly the leader. It didn't seem as though much had changed in fairy order and protocol during the last hundred years. I searched vainly for Bernadette. I didn't recognize any of these fairies. I knew that the average life expectancy of a fairy was around a hundred and fifty to two hundred years or so. At my christening, most of The Seven had been anywhere from seventy-five to a hundred and forty. Bernadette had been the youngest at forty-seven. I had been hoping she would still be here.

"What is it you want?" The head fairy, Alverade was her name, questioned us with cool civility.

"We've come to beg a boon of your fair council," Damien said with a diplomatic bow. When he flashed a smile I saw that they were hardly immune to his charms. The mood lifted significantly.

"This is Princess Aurora Claire of Kalynbrae," he began.

Alverade interrupted him.

"Yes, we know. I'm glad to see that that lunatic Bernadette's gift was successful. Though hardly usual, I must say," she said dryly.

At the mention of Bernadette's name my pulse quickened and I stepped forward eagerly.

"Do you know where she is? Where can we find her?"

"Why in the name of all fairy magic would you want to know that?" she demanded crossly.

"Something happened. Something is . . . wrong. People are starting to fall back to sleep and we cannot wake them," I said.

The room filled with the noise of seven fairies tittering and whispering. I even heard a few giggles, which made me frown. This was no laughing matter. I heard bits of sentences—things like, "I might have guessed" and "I'm not surprised" and "This is just so typical."

"Can you help us or not?" James interrupted, clearly out of patience with them.

"I can't tell you why your kingdom is falling back under that miserable curse of a gift, only Bernadette can do that," Alverade scoffed.

"And where can we find her?" I pressed.

"She's renounced the world and lives as a sort of hermit on Mount Borthwick," Alverade informed us with a look of bored disgust. "Apparently she didn't feel that her *gifts* were appreciated."

"When did this happen?" I asked.

"About fifty years ago, I believe," she answered.

"Will she accept visitors? Is it possible to see her and ask her some questions?" Damien inquired.

"I really could not predict anything that lunatic will do," she said. "You shall simply have to go and see for yourself."

I don't think I remembered fairies being this rude.

James, Damien, and I looked at each other and shrugged. The fairies turned their gazes back to each other and started twittering and whispering and laughing again. None of them acknowledged our presence. It was clear they were done with us.

"Let's go," Damien urged, annoyed, and we all turned and began walking back down the long, sparkling hall toward the main entrance.

"How far is it to Mount Borthwick?" I asked, discouraged.

"Not too far," James assured me, opening the doors for Damien and me. "About a two-day ride and then we'll probably have to hike up the mountain on foot. Horses are easily spooked on that mountain and the trails are narrow."

I looked worried.

"It's not dangerous," he quickly amended. "It's just not ideal terrain for horses, that's all."

Mount Borthwick was the opposite direction from the way we had come so we rode for several hours until we reached a small city called Belgen. Damien was silent for most of the journey. He seemed frustrated and brooding and I wondered what he was thinking about. I realized that I really didn't know him very well for someone whom I was shortly to marry. I suppose he sensed me staring at him because he turned toward me. A wink and charming smile softened my heart and gave me the assurance that I needed.

James took the small purse from Damien and walked into a merchant's shop while Damien and I continued on to the inn at the center of Belgen. It seemed as though word of who we were had spread fast once we left the Fairy Council, because there was something of a hastily put together royal welcome for us when we arrived.

"Prince Damien, Princess Aurora Claire," the innkeeper bowed so low his pointy nose almost touched the wooden floor as brass instruments played a little fanfare. "We are honored to have your patronage at our humble inn."

I glanced at Damien, who looked bored. I nodded to the man graciously and smiled.

"We have prepared our finest rooms for your party," he looked around a bit confused. "I understood that there were three of you . . ." he trailed off.

"Oh yes, my attendant, Sir James, is acquiring supplies and provisions. He'll be here soon," Damien explained with a wave of his hand. "No need to fix up anything special for him. He'll be quite comfortable anywhere. Princess Aurora Claire and I will require your best rooms, however."

I blushed, feeling somewhat embarrassed at Damien's haughty manner. I felt different lately. Almost not like a princess. Almost not like me. Almost like I was just a girl on a long journey, a journey with purpose. Damien's demands reminded me what I was. I didn't really like it. I wanted to pretend for just a little longer.

The innkeeper bowed low again and begged us to follow him, sending out several younger men to take care of our horses.

I smiled again at the man as he stuttered and stumbled nervously through a corridor and long hallway.

"May I inquire as to why we have the honor of your presence here in Belgen?" he asked as we approached two large and ornately carved doors.

"No, you may not," Damien drawled with a yawn. "I can't see how that is in any way your concern."

The poor man turned bright red and coughed and sputtered as he bowed again and again, backing away from us, muttering his apologies.

"Your room, Princess, is here on the right," he gestured and then opened the door wide. I tried to catch his eye so I could somehow reassure him, but he refused to look up.

"I'll send up the cook's finest dishes for your supper," he mumbled, trembling. After he opened Damien's door he bowed again and quickly scurried away.

I looked up at Damien disapprovingly.

"Why, darling, whatever is the matter?" he asked, touching my cheek gently.

"Did you have to be so rude to him?" I asked, pulling away.

He chuckled. "He's a country bumpkin innkeeper who was in awe at seeing royalty. You have been lucky enough to be sheltered from such pesky irritants, but I have dealt with them all my life and have no patience for them."

"He just seemed polite and a bit nervous to me," I argued. I may have grown up spoiled, but I was always polite. Or had that just been my gift of sweetness? I didn't know and that bothered me almost more than the loss of my gifts in general.

Damien's brow darkened for half a second before he pulled my hand to his lips for a tender kiss. "You're right, my darling," he conceded. "I behaved abominably and I'll give him a generous tip as a sign of our gratitude," he said. "Will that make you happy?" He came closer and kissed my forehead.

"Well, yes, I suppose," I said, a little thrown off by his sudden nearness.

"You see? That is why we are such a wonderful pair," he exulted. "Your compassion and sensitivity will always keep me in line." He smiled roguishly and I had to smile in return. "Goodnight, my love," he said as he led me into my room and then retreated with that same grin and closed the door behind him.

"Goodnight," I said to the heavy, wooden door. I was still mildly irritated at his manners, but I liked the idea of him needing me to help him become a better man. I hadn't been needed much in my life and I suppose the romance of the notion appealed to me.

I looked around at my room and was surprised to find that it was really quite lovely. Certainly it was not as luxurious as my quarters back home, but it had a rustically elegant quality and the dark wood gleamed from careful polish and cleaning.

After bathing and changing into a long, comfortable robe, my supper arrived. A shy maid brought in several trays with steaming soup, a roasted chicken, cooked vegetables, and hot bread. There was enough food here to feed several princesses. I ate what I could, but the nervousness about finding Bernadette settled in on me and diminished my appetite. And it was so strangely quiet.

I could hear myself chewing and the fire crackling in the fireplace. That was all.

Thoughts of my mother entered my head. I imagined her falling down as the sleep overtook her and then her attendants, whoever might be left, placing her carefully next to my father. Suddenly I couldn't eat another bite and I got up from my chair, searching for a distraction and finding none.

I opened my heavy door a crack and heard the faint noises of a happy crowd of people, boisterously laughing and talking. I closed it again and sighed as I leaned against it. I didn't feel like being alone. However, it would be highly inappropriate to join Damien in his room or to join the crowd of people out in the inn's dining room. I stewed over it and jumped onto the bed, playing with the fringe on the pillows. The latter seemed like the lesser of two evils.

When had I ever done anything remotely reckless? Besides sneaking around my own palace . . . which hardly seemed reckless at all considering it was my own home. I could cover my face, blend in with the crowd, no one would have to know I was there.

I just couldn't be alone here with my thoughts any longer.

CHAPTER ELEVEN

I had put on my very plainest gown. It was simple dusty blue muslin with a prudish neckline and very little frills. The cut was still fine and the fabric was not cheap, but with my heavy cloak around me, I hoped I could blend in. Not knowing how to do my own hair, I had stuffed it into a dark net. I allowed some pieces to fall forward and shield my face. I studied my reflection in the looking glass. I still looked like me of course, but I didn't think I'd stand out too much. Also, thanks to the faint yet irritating burst of freckles that had taken residence on my nose, I thought I looked much more like a commoner. I took a deep breath to steady myself and then quietly opened my door and slipped out. I tiptoed past Damien's room and down the long hallway toward the noise I could hear at the end of the corridor.

When I turned the corner, I tried to stay close to the wall and slip in unnoticed. The room was bright and warm and full of merry talk and laughter. It smelled of minced meat and pies and dumplings and ale and human bodies full of the scent of work and play. It was a strange yet somehow pleasant sort of combination that filled me with excitement. A few musicians sat in the far corner, plucking out melodies while several men and women sung along. Walking slowly along the wall, I saw an obviously inebriated man cast a bleary gaze in my direction. He then gave me a slow, somewhat sickening smile and I took a step back, deciding to forego my original plan after all.

And then I felt a hand on my shoulder and jumped back, so startled I knocked my head against some hanging antlers on the wall. I whirled around to find James looking down at me.

"What are you doing here?" I gasped, holding one hand to my head where the antlers had bumped me and one on my pounding heart.

"I could ask you the same question," James said with a smirk.

"I just wanted to . . . see what was going on out here," I said lamely.

"Well, as you can see, there's quite a lot going on," he gestured toward the crowded room. I didn't see the disturbing man anywhere. "Anything else?" he asked.

I looked around and chewed on my lip.

James laughed.

"Curious about how the other half lives?"

I thought it would be better if he thought it was merely an aristocratic, snobbish even, curiosity rather than have him realize the truth; that I was desperate to get away from my thoughts and fears. I didn't want to have to talk about it. I wanted to forget about it, if only just for a moment. So I sheepishly nodded and ducked my head.

He shook his head a bit and led me to his table in the corner where we could watch the festivities without being disturbed or attracting too much attention.

"Is there some sort of local holiday or celebration going on?" I asked as I sat back against the sturdy oak bench.

"No, no," James shrugged. "This is a typical night here, I'm told."

"Really?" I was incredulous. "We never act like this at home. Even when there is a ball or royal celebration."

"I bet if you looked down in the kitchen or the servant's quarters you'd find a pretty lively bunch," James said as he took a drink from his tall mug.

"How would you know?" I scoffed. "Knights don't live with the servants." That reminded me of Damien's former thoughtlessness about James's room.

"Where is your room?" I asked without thinking.

James turned his head quickly and looked at me in surprise. I realized how odd that must have sounded, not to mention inappropriate.

"No, I meant . . . that is, I was just curious because Damien said," but then I didn't want to bring up what Damien said either. "I was just . . . wondering how large this inn is." I trailed off.

James seemed somewhat amused by my strange babbling, although still a bit confused at my original question. Where was my gift of wit when I needed it? Gone with my perfect complexion, apparently.

"Well, although I'm not sure how large the inn is, my room is large enough and quite comfortable." He had answered my question in a different way, obviously to save me from more embarrassment. "I assume your rooms are to your liking as well?" he continued.

"Oh, yes. Quite," I mumbled. "So, then . . . the innkeeper must be doing very well for himself." What was I talking about?

"I suppose," James returned, his brow furrowed.

I had no idea how to get out of this conversation.

"Yes. I suppose so. I suppose innkeeping can be a . . . lucrative business venture." I tried lamely, knowing I sounded like a perfect idiot.

James burst out laughing as I hung my head in shame.

"I'm sorry, Your Highness, but I don't know where you're going with this."

"I know, I know," I blushed. "I'm not making any sense." I decided to just leave Damien's name out of it. "I just noticed your room was nowhere near ours and I didn't want you to feel slighted by the distance or distinction or something. You are a knight after all."

James stiffened almost imperceptibly.

"Not that these people are worth anything less than us or, well—" I exhaled loudly, frustrated with my inability to communicate. "I just didn't want you to feel bad." I finished with a slump of my shoulders.

James nodded and sort of smiled. "I assure you that I am completely comfortable and not offended in the least, but I appreciate your concern."

I kept quiet for another moment before leaning forward with my elbows on the table and placing my chin on the palms of my hands. I looked out at the merry little scene before me and said, "Truth be told, I'd rather be closer to all these happy people than cooped up in my quiet, cold room with nothing to think about except who else might be falling back under the sleep."

So much for not wanting to talk about it.

James cast a sidelong glance in my direction before saying, "We'll find Bernadette soon, Claire. And when we do, we'll figure out how to undo this whole thing. Everyone will be fine."

I turned to him in surprise.

"What?" he asked self-consciously, rubbing his face as though at an invisible piece of food when I didn't say anything.

"You called me Claire," I told him finally, still taken off guard.

"I apologize, Your Highness," James said quickly, but I quickly held up a hand.

"No, no, I told you to call me that from the beginning, but you never have before."

"I never thought it appropriate to address royalty by their given names. I guess in this informal setting I slipped."

"Well, I hope you slip more often," I said firmly. "I much prefer Claire to any of those regal titles. Even Aurora. Although Damien seems to prefer it. After all, you have no reason for helping me in this journey other than that you are a good friend to Damien and a generous benefactor to me. The least I can do is let you call me by my given name. I don't think there is any need for formality anymore."

"Well then, I shall try to remember to call you that," he said, avoiding eye contact.

"*Claire*," I said.

"Yes. Claire." He was still looking straight ahead.

"Yes. Good." I smiled and leaned back.

"Would you like another, love?" A pretty young woman holding a pitcher interrupted our silence. She reminded me of several women of the court back home, gazing at handsome men at the balls. I had never bothered looking. What was the point if they would all be gone by the time I awoke from the sleep? Besides, I had the promise of true love's kiss that required no looking or coaxing or even choosing on my part.

"No, thank you," James replied. He gave her a friendly nod, but that was all. She walked away in disappointment.

I chuckled and James looked over in question.

"I think she likes you," I smiled. "You almost broke her heart just then."

"What? No. You don't know what you're talking about," he looked embarrassed.

"Oh, I think I do," I joked. "I think she is just praying that you'll go over and ask her to dance." I gestured over to where she stood near the musicians and several couples who were turning and stomping enthusiastically to the music. She had her eyes fixed on James.

He glanced over quickly before looking back at me.

"I think you are sleep deprived and that we should both get back to our rooms. We have a long journey tomorrow and we'll need plenty of rest."

"Oh that poor, poor girl," I teased with another laugh.

"Come along," James growled, taking my elbow and nudging me forward and off the bench.

I started to walk away as James went to settle his bill. I felt a heavy hand on my shoulder and I spun to find the drunken man who had stared at me earlier standing disturbingly close.

"Pardon me, mistress," he slurred. My stomach roiled at his foul breath. "You don't look half sleepy yet. Care to share a pint with me?"

"Um, no thank you, I was just leaving." I held my face as far away from him as I could.

"Aw, come on, then. One drink couldn't hurt," he insisted.

"I said, no thank you," I grimaced as I tried to shake my arm free.

"Look, I don't take kindly to uppity wenches, even when they're as fine as you are. Perhaps your pride needs to be taken down a notch or two." He leered at me and belched.

"Excuse me, sir," I said firmly in disgust, trying to push my way around him.

"Not so fast, missy. Come on over to my table. My friends and I will show you a real good time and get you feelin' not so high and mighty right quick." He grabbed my arm painfully.

"Please—" I started, still trying in vain to yank my arm away. Suddenly, James reappeared next to me, took hold of my other elbow, and glared at the offensive man.

"Release this young woman at once," he demanded, his tone frigid.

"Who do you think you are to order me about?" the man slurred darkly.

James stepped up to the man who cowered at James's height and he released my arm slowly. James started to lead me away when a massive hand stopped him by jabbing him squarely in the chest.

"Look here," said a giant of a man, spitting tobacco juice out of the side of his mouth. "We don't take kindly to strangers ordering our friends about." The *we* he referred to was he and another man, of equally impressive stature standing next to him. The drunken man regained his swagger now and resumed his leering. James looked cooly at each of them individually, took my arm, and started to lead me past when the one who had been silent so far reached out to grab the back of my gown.

"Don't walk away. We're not done with you yet," he snarled.

Before I could even blink, James had turned and grabbed the man's hand in a death grip. He released my gown as he winced in pain and James quickly spun him around, wrenching his arm behind his back at an unnatural angle. The man wheezed in pain. The other two charged at James just as I jumped out of the way. I saw James quickly jerk the first man's wrist higher until he crumpled onto the floor. The other tall man's fist came crashing toward James's face, but James dodged it and used the other man's momentum to throw him forward and behind him headfirst into a bench. The drunken man foolishly charged and James delivered a quick, decisive blow to the man's chin. His body folded instantly and he fell to the ground. All of this happened in a matter of seconds. I blinked and looked around me, completely dumbfounded, at the three unconscious men.

"Did you kill them?" I gasped.

"They'll be fine," James scowled. "Which is more than they deserve."

James then turned to the crowd and I realized the music had stopped. The innkeeper rushed forward and nearly fell over himself apologizing. I covered my face with my hood in an effort to not be recognized and James hurriedly bid the man good night and apologized for the raucous caused. He then gently took my arm and continued on our original path.

We walked back the way I had come and into the dark corridor beyond the busy room.

"I shall escort you," James said.

"Oh, well, if you don't mind. It's down this hallway," I told him. "It *is* quite dark. I admit I'd appreciate an escort— Wait, hold on. What *was* that back there?" I skidded to a stop and looked up at him, still completely flabbergasted at what had transpired.

"That's what I'm here for," James said as he motioned for me to enter the hallway and I stifled any other questions. I stole sidelong glances at him as we walked. He remained perfectly calm, completely unaffected by the ordeal. I slowed and stopped him again about halfway down the hall. He started to exhale in exasperation, but I held up a hand and said, "I would appreciate it if you didn't mention this to Damien. I mean, I don't want him to think ill of me for . . . venturing off by myself, I guess."

"Oh, of course," James nodded.

We continued walking. My door was several paces past and I stopped again once we reached it.

"Thank you," I whispered. "For . . . everything."

"Good night, Your Highness," he whispered back.

I frowned. "*Claire*," I corrected.

James bowed over my hand and turned around to go back the way we had come. I watched him walk away and then eased the latch to my room open, slipped inside, and locked it securely behind me.

I tried to stop the shivering as I quickly changed into a nightgown, splashed some water on my face, brushed through my hair, and got into bed. I was disturbed by what had happened, naturally, but mostly grateful nothing serious had happened. To me, anyway. Something had definitely happened to those three men. I still couldn't believe it. Those second two men had been enormous. One of them was even larger than James and the other was at least heavier. I couldn't fathom how quickly it had all ended. James had finished it before it had even begun.

No wonder Damien employed him for his protection. I'd never seen anything like it. Sighing and rolling over again, I tried not to imagine the faces of my family and friends as I fought the powerful urge to fall asleep. Each time I closed my eyes the fear that I might not be able to open them again crept in. When I finally succumbed to sleep, I dreamt that the pretty girl in the inn kidnapped James and stole our horses with those vile men from the fight, but I couldn't chase after her because my legs were asleep and I couldn't get them to move.

CHAPTER TWELVE

The next day we ate a hurried breakfast and James went to collect the horses while Damien asked me how I slept.

"I slept well, except for a bad dream," I answered.

Damien remained silent and I realized he was busy smoothing out the cuff of his sleeve. I wondered if he had even heard me.

"It was nothing," I shrugged.

"What? What was nothing?" Damien finally looked over at me. But I couldn't answer because the pretty girl from last night and my dream came around the corner and I suddenly felt silly. Thankfully, James entered right at that moment. For probably the hundredth time, I marveled at how tall he was, especially next to the petite maid. I covered a self-deprecating laugh with my hand as I realized how silly my dream had been. He was much too large for a young girl like that to ever kidnap. James stared at me quizzically. I pretended not to notice.

"The horses are ready, Your Highness," he held open the door. Damien and I walked past him into the courtyard. James helped me mount and Damien led the way through the gates.

We rode hard until the sun set, stopping only twice for water and refreshment. My muscles were still sore, but I could tell I was getting stronger and more resilient, which was pleasing. We camped that night and I slept soundly. It seemed I always slept better when pushed to the brink of exhaustion. The next morning we rode for several hours before coming to the foot of Mount Borthwick. I dismounted and James tied all three horses securely to a group of trees near a pond.

"They'll be fine," James reassured me as he saw me look at Naomi with concern. "Thieves don't venture here because of the mountain's reputation for magic. We'll only be a few hours."

I nodded and smiled, a bit too brightly. I grasped my hands to keep them from shaking.

"Shall we?" Damien gestured with a dramatic flair toward the narrow path ascending the mountain.

We trudged up the mountain toward the haphazard-looking establishment on top. Damien held my hand in his. He said it was to help steady me on the uncertain path, but his smile told me that was not the only reason. James had offered to go first in case of any trickery or unseen danger and he walked briskly a few paces ahead of us. I suppressed a nervous shudder as I realized how close we were to the woman who had saved my life.

"Are you nervous?" Damien asked me. I guess I had not suppressed the trembling as well as I'd thought.

"Yes," I admitted, "I just don't know what to expect. . . . After saving me and the rest of the palace once I can't imagine she would wish to do us ill. But the council made her out to be some sort of lunatic."

Damien tucked my hand into the crook of his arm. "I'm sure she'll have some answers for us. She orchestrated this whole thing, after all."

"Yes, but she really only modified it. Zora was the instigator," I said as the customary and expected sliver of fear and resentment rippled through me at the mention of her name.

"But she is long dead and incapable of hurting you ever again," he assured.

We both slightly quickened our pace to keep up with James, eager to reach Bernadette's dwelling.

When we finally arrived, I saw that it was smaller than I had expected. It was half stone and half wood. There wasn't much reason or order to the structure, with turrets and bay windows at random and a roof that slanted strangely up and then sharply down. It was completely unsymmetrical. Faint smoke came out of an odd chimney pipe that stuck out diagonally from the roof.

James announced our presence by calling out a cheerful, yet slightly cautious greeting.

"Do you think she's home?" I asked when no one appeared.

"The council said she never leaves this mountain, "James responded.

Then I saw something move off to the side of the house. It was a scurrying type of movement. Fast and darting. Damien and James had apparently seen it as well because they both reached for their swords.

"No wait!" I held my hands out to stop them. Something in the blur of movement had caught my attention. A flash of bright, coppery red.

"Bernadette?" I called out. "It's Princess Aurora Claire of Kalynbrae. I've come to beg a favor of you."

"Kalynbrae?" A scratchy, yet oddly whimsical voice came back to us. And then she appeared from behind a woodpile in front of the cottage. Her dark green and gray robes had served as a type of camouflage against the backdrop of shadowy stones and old wood. There was one lock of flaming red hair that had escaped from her cape that had given her away. She looked so shriveled and old, and yet her hair retained its distinctive color that I recognized from the paintings and stories of my past.

She walked slowly toward us and stopped right in front of me. James flinched when she reached out toward my face, but I held out a hand to keep him from interfering. Bernadette stroked my cheeks with her withered hands and looked deep into my eyes.

"Has it really been a hundred years since that night?" she asked, incredulous.

I nodded.

"And here you are. You're alive and well? Did it all work out then?" She had tears in her eyes and I felt a swift, matching response in my own. It must have been ages since she'd received some positive feedback regarding her magic. I hated to disappoint her.

"Yes, I'm fine. This man saved me just as you said he would." I gestured at Damien, who bowed his head slightly in acknowledgement. She looked at him with interest and then glanced at James as well.

On an impulse I reached out to hug her.

"Thank you for keeping them alive," I whispered. "My family; thank you for putting them all to sleep." Of course it had been her. Who else would have taken pity on us like that? She looked a little uncomfortable with my affectionate outburst and mumbled something I couldn't hear as she swiped at her teary eyes.

"So what is it you want?" she asked, her ancient face wrinkling even more as she went back to staring at James and then back at Damien. "Not that I don't appreciate the visit, nor the reassurance that it all worked. But from my experience with the human race, or really any species for that matter, mere gratitude isn't enough to get you to come all the way out to see me on this in the middle of nowhere mountain."

I felt a hot flush of shame that she was right. I would have eventually gotten around to thanking her when things had settled down, I told myself. I hoped I was right.

"It's the sleep," I faltered. "People are starting to— fall back into it . . . And we can't wake them up."

"We need to know why this is happening and what we can do to reverse it. Again," Damien told her.

She stepped back briefly before again taking my face in her hands and staring into my eyes. I felt as though she was searching my soul. I also felt an itch on my nose, but I did my best to ignore it and I believe I only scrunched it a little bit. When she was at last finished she stood back and folded her arms with a look of understanding.

"Well?" I prompted.

"I can see what has happened. Something is not right with the outcome of the spell so it is reversing itself. It can be stopped and made right again only once the spell is correctly completed."

"What does that mean?" I asked. "Will it end when Damien and I get married? Do we need to do something else? Make a public proclamation of some sort?"

To each scenario I posed, Bernadette simply whispered, "Perhaps."

In frustration, Damien demanded, "Do you know what needs to happen? Can you help us at all?"

She looked at him a bit coldly and said, "I have done my best to help the world with my gifts and the world has in turn spurned and rejected me. I refuse to help an unappreciative group of prosaic, bromidic nitwits." She turned to leave and panic flashed through me.

"But *I* never rejected you," I argued, grabbing her sleeve. "How is it fair to punish me for something I never did?"

She paused briefly, then turned toward us once more.

"The only way I will help you is if you prove to me that you are worthy."

"And how are we supposed to do that?" Damien inquired, rolling his eyes.

"You must go on a quest. Through the forest of Foréwald to the very heart and there you will know what you must do to prove yourselves."

She held up her gnarled hands before we could ask any more questions.

"I can tell you nothing else. Now please go."

Her eyes lingered us for one final moment before she jerked away from us and scurried back into her dwelling, shutting the door firmly behind her. Damien ran after her and pounded on the door, demanding more of an explanation. I looked over at James who raised his eyebrows at me and gave a little shrug.

"Damien, it's no use," I called. "She won't do anything she doesn't wish to do. We're lucky she told us as much as she did."

"And exactly how does that information help us?" Damien huffed as he stalked back to me and James. "We're supposed to just march through a cursed forest full of uncharted and mysterious dangers to get . . . What? We don't even know the purpose of this so-called *quest*. This is absolutely ridiculous."

"It's all we can do. We have to try." James said. I looked at him gratefully. Every moment more of my family and friends could be slipping back into the sleep. Although I was still somehow fairly certain I would be last, (I now kicked myself for not thinking to ask Bernadette about that) I had no idea how much time I had.

"How long will it take us to reach the forest?" I asked.

"About a two- or three-days' ride once we get back down the mountain," Damien responded, still glaring back at the cottage.

"We'll camp down where we left our horses," James said, starting back down the path. "It will be dark soon and we can get an early start tomorrow."

The three of us made our way through the brambles and over roots and broken branches, careful to avoid areas with loose gravel. Damien had taken the lead and I noticed that he did not take my hand on our descent, but I reasoned that he must be frustrated and preoccupied with the situation we were in. At one point, my foot slipped on patch of slick, muddy leaves and I stumbled into James's back. He instinctively turned, grasped my shoulders, and steadied me. I thanked him with an awkward smile as he dropped his hands. He kept walking, but did not to get too far ahead of me in case I might need him again. I huffed in frustration under my breath. James glanced at me and waited for me to catch up to him.

"What's wrong? Did you injure yourself when you slipped?"

"No, I'm fine," I sulked. "I apologize that you are continually saving me from my clumsy ways."

"That's what I'm here for," James said in response. I had heard him say that phrase at least once before.

"Well, yes, I'm sure you are, but you don't have to be so arrogant about it." My voice came out sounding extremely petty. I crinkled up my nose in distaste with myself as he gave me look that clearly communicated his confusion at my behavior.

"I'm sorry," I relented. "I'm just frustrated. I'm not used to being so clumsy."

James chuckled. "Did those gifts of yours keep you from falling too?"

"Well, of course," I informed him primly when I realized he was teasing me. "It's my gift of gracefulness. I've never fallen or slipped or tripped or bumped into anyone in my life . . . at least up until last week."

He was quiet for a moment.

"So, even when you were a baby learning to walk you never fell? Not even once?" I couldn't tell if he was making fun of me or genuinely curious, but his question made me laugh.

"I actually don't remember that," I told him. "I assume I took a few spills then, but I'm sure I even tottered gracefully . . . since I'm so graceful, you see." That last bit was said as my foot did a quick double step after faltering over an awkwardly shaped stone. It made me giggle this time instead of frown and huff. James finally gave in a chuckled himself. I had never really joked about my gifts before. It was strangely refreshing.

"Will you two please stop your inane laughter?" Damien shouted over his shoulder. "I hardly think there's anything amusing about our situation."

I bit my lip and glanced at James.

"Since you *were* so graceful, you mean," James whispered with a grin.

I looked at him archly and then smiled back.

CHAPTER THIRTEEN

We made camp quickly that night. James prepared our tents and started a fire while Damien pulled me aside.

"I'm sorry, Aurora, for my frustration earlier," he said penitently. "I'm just so desperate to get this all made right again so we can start our lives together."

I simply nodded my forgiveness. I was tongue-tied again, which was apparently the usual these days.

"The thought of something happening to you is almost more than I can bear . . . I guess I let my fear for your safety get the better of my manners."

My heart softened toward him.

"I understand," I assured him. "And I'm grateful for your concern."

He smiled at me and bent down to kiss my cheek. My heartbeat skittered a bit and we walked back to the fire where James was laying out his bedroll.

"I do feel bad that you don't have a tent, James," I told him.

"Oh, I prefer to sleep under the stars," he answered nonchalantly.

I looked up at the sky and saw the hundreds of twinkling lights. I had to admit that in this warm night air, I'd probably prefer sleeping without a tent as well. However, that was out of the question since it would be hardly appropriate to sleep in the open with two men nearby. I smirked at the irony of that thought. Hadn't I met them both under those exact circumstances?

"They each wished me goodnight as I entered my tent. I could hear their voices low and muted outside my tent as I quickly readied myself for bed. I was exhausted. The two voices started to sound a bit heated, but sleep overtook me before I could give the matter much thought.

The next morning we woke before the sun and got an early start after James had packed up all the belongings and tethered them to his saddle.

"There is one small village on the way to Foréwald," Damien said as he swung up onto his horse. "We'll need to stop there for a meal today and to purchase more provisions for our *quest*." The last word was heavily punctuated by annoyance and sarcasm.

We rode for several hours before taking a break near a stream to water the horses and finish off the food that James had in his knapsack. I sat on the bank, eating an apple and twirling the blades of grass around me with my fingers. Damien lay several yards away with his arms over his eyes, apparently taking a short nap. I looked into the water at my reflection, which was surprisingly clear. And surprisingly disappointing. My hair was tangled and windblown. My cheeks were ruddier than they had ever been. And my nose had another three freckles. That made eight in total. I reached up to touch my face and wiped at a smudge of dirt that was just above my jaw line. I groaned in hopelessness and rested my chin on my arms over my knees as James walked over to me.

"What's wrong?" he asked, sounding partly curious and partly annoyed.

"Do you see this?" I demanded, raising my face to him.

He furrowed his brow. "See what?"

"*This*," I gestured exaggeratedly at my face and hair.

"What? See you? Yes. I see you." James looked puzzled.

I sighed in exasperation.

"No, not just *me*," I grumbled. "It's the way I look."

Now he looked even more confused.

"Do I have to spell it out for you in every humiliating detail?" I moaned, then took a deep breath, resigned to my task, and announced, "I've never looked like this in my life."

It felt like a dramatic moment. At least it did to me. But James quickly shrugged and said, "Oh, that again. Well, I doubt you've ever been on such a rough journey before so it doesn't really count."

"No, no, no," I insisted. "I've gone riding for hours. I've spent all day outdoors. When I was little I even snuck out with the stable hands and played in the mud, for goodness's sake. But I've never looked like this."

"I don't understand. Anyone would look—"

I cut him off. "*Anyone* doesn't fall asleep for a hundred years. Anyone doesn't live with the threat of dying at the age of sixteen hanging over them. *Anyone* doesn't have their entire life spelled out for them and then suddenly not know what in this mad world is supposed to happen next."

James looked briefly taken aback at my outburst. Then he drew his eyebrows together and squinted his eyes in concentration.

"What, so your gifts are your consolation prize for having to go through all of that?" he asked.

"No, of course not," I back peddled. "But—"

"But what? Why do you cling to them?" he pressed.

"They're all I've ever known," I exclaimed.

James realized he'd hit a sensitive spot.

"What are you afraid of?" he asked.

"I don't know," I rolled my eyes. "What if this continues until I'm so ugly that I look like some kind of monster? What if I'll be so clumsy and tongue-tied that I won't be allowed in public? What if I can't speak at all? What if my eyes swell over so that I can't see?" my voice faded to a stop as I realized how ridiculous I sounded.

James smiled patiently at me and then looked out across the stream.

"Look at your parents, Claire. They are a handsome couple and you bear a strong resemblance to both of them. Even without your gifts you would have been born with beauty," James said.

I didn't know how to respond to that at first. I'd never thought of that before. James suddenly seemed uncomfortable at my silence and he cleared his throat awkwardly. Before he could run off somewhere, as he was normally wont to do, I quickly quipped, "That's not necessarily true. From what I've heard of your parents they seem charming and look what happened to you." My response caught him off guard and he laughed.

"When have you ever heard anything about my parents?" he asked, knowing I never had.

"A princess never reveals her secrets," I answered primly.

"Well, it seems that at least your wit isn't completely gone," he chuckled.

No, I thought. Not when I spoke with him. It was only with Damien when I was so overcome with nervousness that I became the stuttering dolt version of myself who I was beginning to resent quite a bit.

"In all honesty," James continued, "I think imperfections are sometimes the best part of people. They are what make people unique."

I interrupted him by saying, "Ah, but you see, it was my perfection that made *me* unique." I smiled to let him know I said it in jest and he shook his head with a rueful smile.

"What's so wrong with freckles? My sister has lots of them and I think they look sweet. I guess I have a soft spot for freckles." His face relaxed when he mentioned his sister. "And as for your hair," he looked down awkwardly, "I think it looks beautiful."

His blatant, earnest compliment so shocked me that I felt my mouth fall open and I had no idea what to say. He cleared his throat again and mumbled something about seeing to the horses before jumping up and briskly walking away.

I stared at my reflection again in the small pool and I tried not to look at my disheveled hair or my freckled skin. What I focused on was the hint of a smile that emerged shyly on my face.

We reached the village in the late morning. James took the horses to a stable while Damien and I went to freshen up at the town's only inn. We met again at the market to purchase supplies and have an early midday meal.

The market was small. There couldn't have been more than twenty stalls. They were selling everything from dried and smoked meats to buttons and spools of thread. There were several beggars sitting under the eaves of buildings. One particularly ragged-looking man stood in the shadows and watched us with hard eyes. I shivered and walked a fraction of an inch closer to Damien and James. This was not a wealthy village by any means. I felt immediately conspicuous with the little jewelry I still wore. The sapphire of my earrings stood out uncomfortably. Even the rich forest green hue of my gown that I had considered modest back home contrasted sharply with the musty browns and grays that the villagers wore. I glanced up at Damien who looked equally uncomfortable. James, thank goodness, efficiently and proactively led the way to the stalls containing the necessary provisions for our journey.

"Quite sad, isn't it?" Damien murmured to me as I was watching James hand a few coins to a man in exchange for a large packet of dried meat.

"What is?" I asked, turning to face him.

"These people," Damien gestured. "This whole place." His look held more disgust than pity.

"Yes, it is sad that they are so very poor. Although they seem to make the best of what they have," I answered gazing at two children giggling over some sort of game involving some old twine and a few sticks.

"I mean, just the general state of filth and poverty," Damien clarified. "I confess I can barely stomach these types of places."

My eyebrows crinkled and I pursed my lips.

"These are your subjects," I stated.

"Yes, of course they are. What of it?"

"Well, forgive me, but shouldn't your attitude, as their sovereign, lean more toward compassion or action than revulsion and disregard?"

Damien was looking at me as though I were a pesky fly that needed to be flicked away. For a moment I wanted nothing more than to *be* flicked away and that frightened me. But then Damien's eyes softened and he threw an arm around my shoulder to draw me nearer to him.

"This is why we are such a perfect pair," he enthused, his eyes sparkling dashingly. "You and I shall lead our kingdom with firmness, fairness, and," he nipped my chin with his finger, "with compassion."

I smiled faintly and distanced myself a little from him, aware that we were drawing even more attention to ourselves.

"I think I'll just go have a look at those carvings over there," I said, squeezing Damien's hand that still held mine before I let it drop to his side.

"Don't be long, love," he cooed.

I shook my head in promise and tried to smile again. I wanted a distraction. I didn't like seeing the cracks in my perfect prince's personality. But that's what they were. Cracks. Occasionally I caught these glimpses that I didn't . . . Well, I didn't really like them at all. I ducked my head down and walked quickly to the cart. It held small wooden figurines and tokens and stood several stalls away from where James and Damien stood sorting through fruits and grains. The carvings became more and more impressive the closer I came. The artist obviously had great skill. The wood gleamed from careful sanding and polishing. One small figurine caught my special attention. It was of a beautiful young maiden, asleep against a soft cushion. I marveled at the detail and exactness. The maiden's long hair curled out and around her sleeping form. Her face looked peaceful, wistful even. As though she couldn't wait to see what would happen when she woke up while at the same time a little afraid of it. I smiled and blushed as I realized I was foolishly projecting my own feelings onto the small wooden statue.

"Do you like it?"

I jumped at the question. The young man standing behind the cart was smiling at me. He was extremely handsome and had a calm, confident air about him.

"Yes, it is very beautiful," I said. "Are these yours?" I asked, gesturing at the figurines. "I mean, did you make them?"

He nodded proudly in response. "It was just something of a hobby, but recently my grandfather encouraged me to try to sell them."

"I'm so glad he did," I told him. "You have a real gift."

"Thank you, but it seems not very many people have the money for such luxury items. At least not here."

"Have you tried selling them in bigger towns and cities?" I asked.

"Yes, a few. I come from a town not far from this one where they became quite popular, and I plan to keep selling them at different markets I travel to."

"Well, you've found a loyal customer in me," I smiled. "I'll take that sleeping maiden there."

"An excellent choice, my lady," he said, wrapping the figurine with flare as I pulled out my small purse from a hidden pocket along the side of my cape. I handed him the amount he asked for and reached out to take the statue, now wrapped in felt and canvas.

"You know, that isn't one of my popular subject for carvings, although it is a personal favorite. It comes from a legend, passed down in my family, of a girl who was forced to sleep for a hundred years after pricking her finger on the thorn of a rose."

I nearly dropped the statue.

Before I could ask him more I felt a rough hand seize my arm and yank me toward a dark, hooded figure. I gasped and looked up in panic to see the man with hard eyes who I'd spied earlier.

"Hand over yer purse," he growled as he wrapped his other hand around my throat.

I screamed but was quickly cut off by the man's filthy hand over my mouth. The stench from his breath made me gag and my heart threatened to leap out of my chest.

"Let her go!" demanded my new artist friend. He darted around the stall and my attacker yanked me closer to him bruising the tender skin around my neck. What happened next was so quickly and efficiently done I hardly realized what was happening. Somehow, the artist managed to kick the attacker in the shins, pull me away from him, and then hit the grimy man squarely in the jaw in what seemed like one fluid motion. The vile man went down, groaning and holding his broken face.

My rescuer steadied me and looked worriedly at my face. Before he could ask me if I was alright James and Damien rushed up, breathless and furious.

"Claire, are you alright?" James asked.

"What happened, darling?" Damien asked.

"Claire, who was that?"

The incessant questions and rapidly growing amount of spectators swirled around in my ears and vision. *Oh no*, I thought. *Please don't.*

I did.

I fainted.

To put it poetically, I swooned. My world blackened.

Chapter Fourteen

How utterly humiliating, was my first coherent thought. I was really starting to hate the weakness I was constantly putting on display for the entire world to see.

"She's coming around." That was James's voice.

"Move out of my way. Let me see her." That was Damien's.

I struggled to open my eyes and saw two concerned faces a mere arms length from my own. I winced and closed my eyes again.

"I'm fine," I muttered and shut my eyes again with a groan.

"Darling," that was Damien again. "Drink this water. You've had a terrible shock."

"Yes, I know," I grumbled. "I was attacked and nearly strangled to death." I grimaced. That wasn't *quite* true. That horrible beggar had only put his arm around my neck, but I thought that making it sound more than it actually was would make my pitiful fainting spell less shameful. Actually, my artist friend had put a stop to everything before much of anything could even happen. My artist friend—

I started to sit up but the pounding in my head and Damien's hands forced me back down. Where was my mysterious savior? Where was the man who had carved my story and called it a family legend?

"That man saved me," I told James and Damien. "Where is he?"

"He's in the dining hall," James told me, gently putting a fresh wet towel on my forehead. "He's waiting to see you."

"Dining hall?" I asked groggily. "Where are we?"

"The Inn," he explained.

"How long was I . . . unconscious?" I asked, embarrassed.

"Only a few minutes, my pet," Damien assured me. I looked suspiciously at James who nodded in confirmation.

"And the thief?" I asked apprehensively.

"Locked up, safely away from you and subject to the punishments of the law," Damien cooed and I nodded.

"I'd like to see him now," I told them.

"That wretched mongrel?" Damien was incredulous, but James understood.

"She means the wood carver," he told Damien, reaching to help me sit up. "Are you sure you're ready to stand?" he asked me.

"Of course," I brushed him away and forced my spinning head to still itself and planted my feet solidly on the ground. I wasn't as steady as I would have liked, but it would have to do. We made our way into the dining hall—it was more of a room—and I quickly spotted my friend at a corner table, toying with a slice of thick, dark bread. He stood as soon as he saw us enter.

I rushed over to him and took his hand in my own.

"Thank you for helping me," I said, bowing my head slightly. "I am forever indebted to you for your quick action and bravery."

The man looked a little embarrassed at my display so I toned it down a little.

"Let us purchase you a good meal. It really is the very least we can do," I tried. I needed to talk to him.

"It was really nothing," he insisted.

"On the contrary," I enthused. "Here, we'll all eat together." I sat down next to him and motioned for James and Damien to do the same. I could sense that my companions were itching to be on the road again since we had a long ride ahead of us, but I needed to hear more about this man's family legend that just happened to be my life's history, more or less.

"First of all," I said cheerfully, "I don't even know your name."

"It is Grégory, my lady," he answered.

"It is truly a pleasure to make your acquaintance," I returned. "I'm Claire and these gentlemen are Damien, my fiancé, and his truest friend, James." I could tell Damien almost chafed at the omission of our titles, but I ignored it. Grégory nodded a modest greeting to all of us.

"So," I said in a friendly tone, "You were telling me the history behind the lovely figurine I purchased before that . . . that man interrupted us."

"Um, yes," he stuttered. "It is a family legend. It was passed down from my great-great-grandfather. I'm told he was always a little eccentric and he tried to pass the story off as truth. It became a favorite bedtime story in our family although we were teased in the village for having a crazy ancestor. I've always had a soft spot for the romance and mystery of the story. I suppose that's why I choose to carve it so often."

The moment he mentioned a great-great-grandfather my heart began to pound wildly. When he said this man thought of the story as the truth it nearly leaped out of my chest. *Could it be?*

"What was your great-great-grandfather's name?" I asked breathlessly.

"Alvere," he answered, puzzled.

I felt tears spring to my eyes. Oh, Angeline. My poor, sweet friend. So he hadn't been able to return in time. Although unlikely, I had held some small hope that he could somehow be found on the palace grounds, detained by who knows what, but alive and well and in love with Angeline. Now that hope was gone.

"Is something wrong, my lady?" Grégory asked me, concerned by my intense reaction to what he considered a simple fable.

I threw a look at Damien and James who both communicated warning in their eyes.

Caution be hanged.

"What if I were to tell you that your story isn't just a story . . . That it really and truly happened almost exactly as you said?"

Grégory looked at me dumbfounded and a bit suspicious and then glanced at Damien and James.

"I suppose I'd ask you to stop mocking me. I've been teased enough for this story and my crazy family."

"Really, Grégory," I pleaded. "I'm the princess who pricked her finger on a thorn—it was a spindle actually, but our palace was surrounded by rose thorns for the hundred years so I can see where the mix up happened—and this man" I gestured at Damien "woke me with true love's kiss."

"Please stop," Grégory sounded annoyed now.

As my last resort I asked if the maiden in his story had a name.

"Yes, she did, and it wasn't Claire," Grégory retorted.

That was strange. I wracked my brains for variations of my name that it might have morphed into throughout the generations of telling and retelling. Then suddenly I knew.

"Was it Angeline?" I whispered.

Grégory's face paled a little. "You might have heard the story before," he argued hesitantly.

"Do you know what he, Alvere that is, looked like? Did your grandfather perhaps ever describe him?"

"Yes," he responded. "Almost everyone in my family is artistic. We have simple portraits of everyone."

"Well then, let me describe him to you and tell me how I would know that." I pictured Alvere in my head for a moment. I had to get this right.

"He had wavy, dark brown hair that curled a bit around his forehead and over his ears that stuck out just a little. His eyes were a grayish-green that sparkled when he laughed. His nose crinkled a bit when he smiled and he had a strong rounded jaw. His skin was almost olive in complexion and he was tall and lean." I opened my eyes and stared into Grégory's own astonished eyes, also grayish-green.

"You know, you look a bit like him yourself."

"How can this be possible?" he breathed the question.

"Angeline is one of my lady's maids. She and Alvere were deeply in love and they were engaged to be married. My entire kingdom fell asleep and woke up when I did, only Alvere was away at the time performing a trade for my father. Remarkably, he was the only one in our closest circles who was away at the time."

"So he wasn't crazy?" Grégory breathed.

"No, just tragically separated from his true love."

"He . . . married. I mean, I wouldn't be here if he hadn't. Although I always heard that he was a melancholy sort of person . . . I guess now I know why."

I hadn't thought of that. That is, I hadn't dwelled on that part of Grégory's family history. The part that means that Alvere moved on and married someone else. He was so young. Of course he would have found love again. It still stung a little. A betrayal to my only friend. At least he never forgot her.

"I don't think I would have been able to find love again if such a thing had happened to me," Grégory said, more to himself than any of us. That's when I had a sudden, splendid idea.

"Grégory, I have had a sudden inspiration," I told him, my voice growing excited. "Would you perhaps journey to my home and bring word to them of our progress?"

"Progress?" he asked.

Oh, of course he had no idea what we were doing here. I told him of the spell and the relapse and our quest to find the final cure. I even told him about my other gifts and how they too were fading.

"I used to be quite beautiful," I bemoaned, tossing a long, golden curl.

Grégory looked confused. Damien nodded loyally. James rolled his eyes and blew out his breath.

"Used to be?" Grégory asked. "I don't understand."

"And you never will," James shook his head.

I ignored both of them and went on with my request.

"If you would bring news to my palace, we would finance your journey of course, I would be forever grateful and in your debt." My smile faltered momentarily. "I suppose I'm already forever in your debt for earlier today, but now I'll be forever and eternally and always in your debt."

"Please stop," Grégory held up his hands. "I'll be happy to go."

"And you'll find Angeline and tell her . . . personally . . . what happened to Alvere?"

Grégory nodded solemnly.

I smiled sadly, but with the sadness there was also hope.

We saw Grégory off, loaded with supplies for the journey and a few silver coins in his pocket. I had quickly scribbled a note to my mother, refusing to consider the possibility that she was no longer awake, and I gravely handed it to Grégory.

"Please see that this reaches the queen," I told him. "And good luck. Have a safe journey."

"Thank you, Your Highness," Grégory said quietly, aware of our attempts to disguise our identities. "And good luck on your journey as well."

"Thank you," I smiled and watched him as he rode away, driving his cart out of the market place.

"Claire, really, we've lost a lot of daylight because of this delay," Damien said, drawing me toward him. "We must leave as soon as possible."

I nodded in agreement and we walked to our horses. James's horse was loaded up with sacks full of supplies. I mounted Naomi and nudged her gently to fall in line after Damien. After a few minutes, James rode up beside me.

"I'm glad you were able to send word back to your home," he said.

"Yes, he seems a very trustworthy and capable individual, doesn't he?" I responded.

He nodded.

"Of course, you realize I have ulterior motives for this little errand," I smiled mischievously.

He glanced over, one eyebrow raised.

"He's perfect for Angeline," I explained. "If anyone can help her get over the loss of Alvere, it will be him. I'm sure of it."

James shook his head. "I should have known," he said with a smile.

"Yes, you should have," I laughed. "In the first place, you now know me well enough that you should have realized I would come up with such a brilliant plan as this. And in the second, you're an intelligent person . . . I'm surprised you didn't see it yourself. But then, you're hardly the romantic that I am."

James laughed again. "Most definitely not."

I tossed my hair over my shoulder and smiled coyly. Old habits are hard to break, I suppose. A little embarrassed at my brazen flirting with my fiancé's knight I ducked my head to cover a blush and nudged my horse up to ride closer to Damien. But not before I saw James shake his head with a grin.

CHAPTER FIFTEEN

*T*hat evening I sat idly looking at the fire. Damien was off washing up while James unpacked our supplies. The flames were steady and the embers glowed and crackled. Now that the excitement of finding Grégory had worn off, I found myself dwelling on the beggar's attack from earlier. I didn't think it had been that big of a deal at the time. Apart from the embarrassment at fainting, the whole ordeal was over and done with almost before it began. And yet my mind kept returning to it. It disturbed me to a great degree. I mulled it over in my mind. No one had ever attacked me before. Not physically. I had only ever had to worry about my long sleep, never a physical assault. Even Zora had used her powers to mentally, hypnotically draw me in; she hadn't used brute force to overpower me. The man had attacked me because he could see that I had money. It wasn't a personal attack. So why was I so disturbed? Grégory had disposed of the wretched thief quickly and efficiently. But for that split second, I hated how helpless and panicked I'd felt. I hadn't had the slightest notion of how to defend myself. I sighed heavily.

"What's wrong, Claire?" James asked, not looking up from where he knelt rolling out the bedrolls.

"Nothing," I evaded.

He shrugged. I sighed again. Loudly.

James stopped what he was doing and looked up at me in exasperation. Then he saw my expression, which must have looked appropriately crestfallen, and immediately came a little closer to where I sat.

"We won't let anything like what happened this morning ever occur again." He sounded full of regret and shame. "After all, that's what I'm here for." He attempted a half-smile, which I answered with one of my own. That repeated phrase was starting to grow on me.

"That's not it, exactly," I murmured. How did he always seem to know what I was thinking?

He waited for me to say more.

"It's just . . . that I felt so—helpless," I said dejectedly. "I hate that. I'm so—I'm so tired of it."

"I should have been there," he muttered.

"No, I mean, I should have seen it coming or defended myself better. Something." I was exasperated and hopeless. I suppose I would always need someone to save me.

"I know I've never really left the castle before now, but well, I'm over one hundred years old. I should have a little more worldly wisdom about me." I huffed, even as I joked about my age. James rewarded my weak attempt at humor with a small smile. He was quiet for a moment. Then abruptly, he turned to me.

"You know, there are a lot of things you could have done to protect yourself that would be easy, almost instinctual," James told me.

"Like what?"

"Well, obvious things like scratching, pulling away, even biting or going for his eyes," he explained.

"His eyes?" I made a face. "I don't know if I could do that. Besides, he had a knife!"

James leaned back on his heels and looked at me for a moment before standing up and walking over to me.

"Here, stand up," he held out his hand to help me.

"Why? What are you going to do?" I asked.

"I'm just going to show you a few things that you can do if you ever happen to be in a similar situation."

My mouth dropped. "What? How?" I demanded.

"It's easy," he explained, pulling me up and over to an empty space. "If someone is coming at you from in front of you, you can try this."

He took my hand and formed it so only my pointer and middle finger were extended.

"Now, you place these fingers here," he said, placing them at the base of his throat, between his collarbones. "Now push me back. Hard." I did so and he moved away.

I rolled my eyes. "You don't have to go *so* easy on me," I said wryly.

"No, really," he insisted. "That's all the strength it takes to at least slow them enough to run away."

"So, I really pushed you away, just like that?" I asked.

He nodded, smiling. I grinned. And then I came at him again.

"Of course, if you move that slowly I'll have plenty of time to do this." He smiled arrogantly as he blocked my arm and swiftly moved it behind me and twisted me around until I found myself in a tight grip from behind. I blinked stupidly, then finally tugged my arms away and he released me immediately. I turned back around to find his face still hosting a smug grin, apparently delighted to have the upper hand.

"Alright, alright, sir," I nodded with a sarcastic display of respect. "Not so slow. Got it. Now show me another one," I grinned.

He then taught me to push up on the bony underside of the nose, which produced a similar effect. We ran through that movement a few times and my excitement with my impromptu self-defense lesson caused me to get a little carried away and I ended up hitting him so hard his eyes began to water.

"I'm so sorry," I crowed gleefully.

"I'm sure you are," he said dryly, holding his nose and blinking rapidly. "You look very upset."

"But what if he comes at me from behind? Like at the market." I asked, too excited to acknowledge his comment.

"Well, you could try stomping down on his foot or elbowing him hard in the stomach," he suggested.

I nodded eagerly and waited for him to show me, but he didn't move.

"Come on," I insisted. "Let me practice."

"I don't think so," he laughed. "I'm not letting you get anywhere near my feet or stomach after what you just did to my nose."

"Don't be such a baby," I teased, motioning for him to attack me. I turned my back to him and waited. After a moment's hesitation I heard him take a few steps before I felt his arms encircle me in a tight grip.

"So now I just stamp down on your foot, right?" I asked as I lifted my right leg and then stomped down as hard as I could.

James let out a surprised and quickly suppressed grunt of pain and stumbled back. I whirled triumphantly to find him holding his foot. His face was remarkably red.

"I thought we were just practicing," he protested.

"I'm sorry this time. I really am," I placated, coming closer and patting his shoulder. "But can we try it just one more time so I can elbow you in the stomach?" I tried smiling beguilingly and James turned red again before stuttering that one more time would be fine if I didn't elbow him as hard as I could.

I agreed and turned away from him again. This time, James hesitated a bit longer before slowly bringing his arms around me and pulling me toward him until my back was against his chest. I suddenly felt embarrassed and shy and forgot what I was supposed to be doing. I knew he was tall and broad and, well, impressively strong in general, but knowing by seeing was an entirely different thing from knowing by feeling. My mouth went dry and I struggled to put a sentence together.

"Um . . ." I said stupidly. "So now I just . . ." I trailed off again and tilted my head around to look up at his face. His blue eyes seemed very dark and while he didn't exactly look mad, he was very tense and I stared in curious fascination as that muscle in his jaw flinched.

"What's going on here?" a crisp voice demanded.

I leapt out of James's arms and we both turned to see Damien standing a few feet away, arms folded across his chest, head cocked to one side.

"Oh, Damien," I exhaled. "You startled me. James was just teaching me how to defend myself incase I'm ever attacked again like I was at the market yesterday."

James just stood with his arms behind his back, staring at the ground. Those jaw muscles were hard at work again, clenching and unclenching.

Damien laughed and came closer to me, dragging me into his arms. "My darling Aurora," he cooed. "You won't ever need to do any of these silly maneuvers. You'll always have someone close by to protect you."

He turned to James. "I don't think any more of these *lessons* will be needed, James," he said, his emphasis causing me to blush for some reason I didn't quite understand.

James nodded curtly and said, "Of course, Your Highness."

"Oh, but really, it was so helpful—" I tried starting again, but Damien interrupted me.

"Come along, darling," he smiled, pulling my hand. "I wanted to show you these beautiful flowers I saw by the stream."

I went with Damien, but turned back to mouth a "sorry" to James. I don't know if he saw me or not, but he didn't acknowledge my apology, instead he simply got back to working on clearing our campsite.

The wildflowers weren't really that much to look at, just little blue and white blooms along the stream's edge, but I praised them admiringly for Damien's sake. For a moment, after staring at the flowers for a while, I thought he might take me in his arms, but he only held my hand again and led me back to camp. James treated both of us to a stony silence for the rest of the evening. I felt miserable, but I really wasn't sure why. Eventually I retired to my bedroll and tried to put the entire experience out of my mind. Sleep came eventually. And mercifully, I did not remember dreaming.

The next morning James retained his chilly demeanor. He ignored me through breakfast and silently packed my things onto Naomi. James left to fill our water canteens in the river and after stealing a glance at Damien, who looked bored and distracted by something on his sleeve, I followed him. I jogged to catch up to James. Once I reached him, I simply walked near his side and stole a sidelong glance at him. He stubbornly refused to meet my gaze. I cleared my throat once, then again for emphasis. James looked pointedly away.

"Come now, James," I cajoled. "You can't stay angry at me forever."

He finally looked at me just as I tripped on my hem and caught myself before I could fall flat on my face. His arms went out instinctively. My clumsiness was becoming somewhat expected. But I righted myself before he needed to catch me and his arms fell back to his sides. I could tell he was fighting a smile so I wiggled my eyebrows and gave him a silly grin. He finally gave in and the corners of his mouth reluctantly turned up.

"You really are the most insufferable princess," he shook his head at me.

I frowned thoughtfully and tapped my chin. "I don't remember that being one of my gifts . . ."

James smothered a laugh under his breath and then proceeded to list all of the irritating things I had done lately to illustrate the fact. When I just kept smiling at him he stopped his rant to shake his head again.

"I'm telling you how awful you are," he explained, laughing now. "Why do you look so happy about it?"

"No one has ever pointed out my flaws before. This is fascinating. Please, go on." I said, pretending seriousness.

He laughed again and I joined him.

"Actually, I'm just glad you feel comfortable enough to tease me—because I know teasing was all you were doing since I *am* perfect," I said with a mischievous look. "Or I will be once I get my gifts back."

James snickered.

"This means we're friends, right?" I asked him. I retained my playful tone, but I was actually nervous to hear his answer. I had so little experience with friendship.

He gave me an odd look. "Um . . . yes. I suppose we are," he said.

"Well then," I beamed.

"Well then," he echoed. And then he was smiling and shaking his head again.

CHAPTER SIXTEEN

We rode for the rest of the day and reached a small clearing near a stream by late afternoon. I dismounted and led Naomi to the water. I stroked her neck a few times and whispered a few words of encouragement and thanks in her ear before kneeling by the stream's edge. My cupped hands brought cool water to my eager lips and I gulped the water with an exuberance that would have made my governesses scold. Damien and James performed similar actions a few yards downstream.

"How much further until we reach the forest?" I called over to them.

"Not long, my love," Damien answered. "An hour at most."

I nodded and lay back in the tall grass. I gazed at my hands against the backdrop of the sky. The blueness of the sky always astounded me. It was difficult for me to understand where the color comes from. How is such a perfect, clear blue formed?

James appeared over me and I squinted up at him expectantly.

"Don't tell me," he smirked. "Your hands used to be perfectly smooth and they were the most perfectly formed hands in all the land."

"Well, yes, as a matter of fact, they were," I smiled. "But that's not what I was thinking about."

He plopped down next to me and mimicked my position with his hands held out above him.

I turned my head to look at him.

"Where's Damien?" I asked, fighting the blush I felt coming on at how close his face was to mine.

"Who knows," he said, glancing at me before quickly looking back at his hands. "Primping, most likely," he finished disinterestedly.

I couldn't hold back a giggle.

"So what are we looking at?" he asked me.

"The sky," I informed him.

"And our hands?"

"Mmm. I enjoy the contrast."

"The contrast?"

"There's something fascinating about the solid, sort of heaviness of our hands and skin next to the wispy depths of sky," I explained. "I mean, we're so . . . real. The sky is just there, but it isn't somehow. You can never touch it. You might climb the highest mountain, but it's always higher. Around you, but still apart. We're in the very midst of it, and yet, it's unattainable."

I glanced at James who looked like he was trying to focus. He closed one eye and said, "Yes, I can see what you mean."

"And that blue," I breathed. "Can you think of anything else that comes close in rivaling that beauty? The depth and density of it always astonishes me. The air around us is transparent, but up there, it turns into something wonderful. Somehow it absorbs the reflections of everything and becomes such a blue it . . . it takes my breath away."

James was silent for a long moment. I started to feel a little ashamed of my fanciful musings. Then James turned and propped himself up on his elbow.

"When did you become so philosophical?" he asked with a smile, but there wasn't any teasing in that smile.

I gave in to the blush and smiled back. "Well, as I've said before, I really am very old," I laughed. "Much older than you, anyway, by nearly a hundred years."

His laughter joined my own and I held my hands up once more.

"So real," I murmured. "I'm real and I'm here."

James dropped back onto his back after another minute only he put his hands under his head instead of extended out in front of him.

"Of course you're real."

"I know, but sometimes it doesn't quite feel like it. Or maybe it feels too real." Now it was me who turned to look at him. "Before the sleep, my life was like a fairytale. I don't mean that it was all wonderful," I shook my head, "I mean that it was planned. It had an *ending. I* had an ending. Everything was muffled, a little hazy through the veil of my eventual *end*. Now, it's as if I'm living for the first time. Free to do whatever I want. Free to not know what will happen next. And while that terrifies me a little, I like it. It's just so—so very real."

James sat up and looked down at me. He then stood and reached down for my hands to pull me up beside him.

"So you like not knowing what will happen next?" he asked.

I nodded, hesitantly. "I didn't think I did. In fact, at first I hated it." My voice trailed off and I shrugged. "But now, yes. I think I am starting to enjoy it quite a bit."

"Well then," he said, all business. In the next moment, he swept me off my feet and dumped me in the water. I yelped in surprise as I flailed my arms before landing with a splash. I came up sputtering.

"How dare you," I gasped, struggling to find my footing. James threw his head back and laughed.

"I thought you are supposed to be saving me, protecting me. Isn't that *what you're here for*?" I turned his words against him as I tried to wipe water from my eyes.

He only laughed and said, "Yes, that is what I'm here for. I'm also just helping you in your pursuit of the unplanned and unexpected. Not to mention . . . but now I'm going to mention it —sorry—you needed a bath anyway." He finished this statement with a smirk, which showed he knew exactly how that type of remark would be received.

I shrieked in outrage as I lunged up the bank, grabbed his hand and yanked him toward me. Startled, he tumbled past me and into the water himself. He came up laughing and I laughed with him before splashing him eagerly in the face.

"And just what are you two halfwits about now?" Damien asked as he walked into the clearing toward us.

"Just cooling off," I crowed, directing a splash his way that caught him full in the chest.

"For goodness's sake, Aurora," he complained, but he was smiling too.

We reached the forest sooner than I would have liked. As much as I was in a hurry to find out what the cause of the relapse was, I had heard terrifying stories of this place since I was a little girl. By the reactions of Damien and James when they heard our destination, I don't think much had changed regarding its reputation in the last hundred years. It was nearly sunset, so we decided to camp just outside of the forest's limits so that we could have an early start the next day. James built the fire and I offered to organize our dinner. I felt that I was getting rather good at arranging a meal out of basically nothing, at least by palace standards.

I took a few pieces of dried meat and fruits as well as the few fresh loaves of bread we had purchased and set them carefully out on our thin metal trenchers. Compared to the dishes we used at the palace, they seemed terribly rustic and heavy. How would James continue to carry them without his horse?

"You know, you really should leave these dishes with the horses tomorrow. We can make do without them, I'm sure, and they seem very heavy, thin as they are." I brushed some leaves off a flat rock and put the said trenchers around it, pretending it was a dining table. I could almost hear James smile and then I definitely heard him laugh.

"Thank you for your permission, Your Highness," he said as he blew on the small beginnings of a campfire. "I had already considered that. Don't worry. We'll only take the essentials."

I felt a little flustered that what I'd thought was thoughtful was instead very obvious.

"Oh, yes, of course. How silly of me. Of course we won't take them. I just wanted to make sure . . ." I trailed off in embarrassment.

"No, really, Claire. Thank you for thinking of that. That was kind of you."

I nodded, feeling better.

Damien came up from the creek and sat on a rock near the food and took his meal eagerly. "You can't imagine how starving I am," he said between carefully and properly chewed mouthfuls.

I thought I probably could since our eating patterns had been identical for some time and I was starving myself. I waited for James to finish the fire and then handed him his trencher.

"Thanks," he nodded.

"Of course," I smiled.

The meat had excellent flavor. And my apricots and figs were delicious. It must have been a good market despite the poverty.

"Well," Damien said as he finished his meal. "I'm going to lie down for a bit. Relax before bed." He went over and entered his tent as I called out a good night to him.

James took a bit longer to eat and then started gathering the dishes to go down to the stream.

"I can do that," I offered, standing quickly.

"Are you sure?" James seemed surprised.

"Yes, of course. I may have never washed my own dishes before, but I'm sure it cannot be *that* complicated."

"I'll carry them down to the stream for you," he offered.

We walked the short distance to the water and both knelt down at the edge. I tentatively took a trencher and dipped it in the water. James took another and gave it a good dunk and scrub. I followed his example and the plate quickly became clean. Of course, since we were eating dry foods it wasn't that dirty to begin with. We finished quickly and headed back to camp. I could hear Damien lightly snoring from inside his tent. James walked to his knapsack and packed a few things before cinching it closed. He started to walk off and I quickly followed him.

"Where are you going?" I asked.

"I have to set a few snares before I sleep. We weren't able to get as much dried meat at that market as I wanted. I want to get some fresh meat for tomorrow morning. Who knows what kind of wildlife we'll find in the forest."

I must have looked terrified because he quickly amended the statement.

"I mean, of course we'll be fine. Don't worry." He strode off and I bit my lip before running after him.

"Can I come?" I asked. "I've never set a snare before."

He gave me an odd look.

"Well, yes, I supposed that should be obvious. But you never know. You didn't expect me to have stolen knifes from servants, did you?" I said proudly.

"You bring that up a lot," James said over his shoulder.

I huffed in irritation. "Well, can I come or not?" I nearly whined before catching myself.

"I doubt I could stop you, short of tying you down, which I don't think you or Damien would look kindly upon. So, sure, be my guest."

I beamed and fell into step beside him.

"Luckily for you, and for me, you don't have to be that quiet when laying snares. If we were hunting, I would have never agreed to you coming."

"Are you implying that I am loud, sir?" I asked, fighting a smile.

"Oh, was I only implying? I'll try and be less subtle next time," he quipped.

We walked in companionable silence until we reached a clearing James deemed acceptable for his snares. He showed me how to bend and fasten the branches and how to lay the parts just so. As we stepped back and examined our handiwork, I suddenly felt short of breath.

"What's wrong?" James asked.

"I don't know," I started. "I just thought all of the sudden, 'what am I doing out here?' and I didn't quite know how to answer the question."

My hands started shaking and I clasped them tightly. I turned to leave and I tripped on a root, landing on my knees before James could catch me. He quickly helped me up and placed a finger under my chin to tilt my face up. His face held no judgment, only concern.

"Are you alright?"

I tried to regulate my breathing. I was taking in too much air.

"Um, yes, of course. I just— I just . . . I'm sorry. I suddenly have no idea who I am." I forced a nervous laugh that came out a bit too brightly.

James remained quiet and I continued to stare at my shaking hands.

"Look, my hands. They won't stop shaking. Why won't they stop?" I looked up at James for the answer.

He simply took my hands in his and rubbed them in his own. We stood like that for several minutes, him warming my hands, me copying his steady breathing. And then the anxiety was gone. I pulled my hands slowly away and looked at him gratefully, although I was embarrassed.

"Thank you," I said quietly. "I'm not sure what came over me there."

"Don't be ashamed," James insisted kindly. "You've been on a long, hard journey. We're about to enter an enchanted forest. You have more at stake here than any of us. And, you're also coming to terms with new aspects of your personality that you have never had to deal with before. All at the same time. Give yourself a break." He looked down quickly and then continued. "I think you're doing an incredible job of it."

I didn't know what to say. I felt such gratitude that *thank you* seemed hardly adequate.

"Come, let's get you back to camp. We need to rest up before tomorrow." He took my hand and pulled me back to our tents.

I bid him good night, smiled gratefully, and tried to sleep.

The next morning we rose early. James went out to retrieve any catches in his snares. There was no wall or fence or hedge or anything to mark the beginning of the forest, but somehow the change was obvious. The trees looked blacker, thicker, and more menacing. The foliage was less whimsical and more foreboding. Everything looked scratchy and tangled in general and there wasn't a hint of a wildflower.

James sensed my fidgety hesitation and turned to me. "It'll be fine. I—We're trained for this sort of thing."

I considered the subtle change of pronouns as I gave him a grateful smile. Damien stepped closer to me and placed an arm possessively around my waist.

We had to tie up the horses near the stream. Damien informed me that people never brought animals into the forest. Especially horses as they are easily startled and that kind of reaction to surprises is never good in a forest full of the unknown. I didn't feel comfortable leaving Naomi alone, but James assured me that that there was plenty for them to eat and drink and we should only be in the forest for a couple days. James took only the essentials off his horse and strapped them onto his own back. He then walked to the edge of the forest and entered after only a moment's hesitation. I supposed there was no point in wasting any more time. I squared my shoulders, took a deep breath, and took a step. One step turned into two, which turned into three and then four. This wasn't so very hard. Damien stood close by at my left and James walked a few paces in front.

After what seemed like several uneventful minutes, I accidentally brushed a hanging vine as we passed through a narrow cluster of trees. The vine flew up as though suddenly caught up in a gust of wind, but I felt no breeze. It lashed toward me and snaked itself around my wrist. I cried out, yanking my arm away, but the vine held fast. James darted toward me and quickly cut the branch with a knife that seemed to appear out of nowhere. The vine instantly released me and fell limply to my side. I gasped in relief and stared at James and Damien. I was frightened to see their equally shocked expressions. James returned his knife to the sheath hanging at his belt, concealed by his leather tunic.

"Are you alright?" my two companions asked simultaneously. I gulped and nodded.

"We'll walk single file from now on," James advised. "And be careful not to touch anything."

The next hour seemed to go on for days. I walked painstakingly carefully, suppressing my nervousness and the painfully strong instinct to turn and run in a mad dash out of the forest. My muscles began to ache from the effort. I kept my eyes on James, trying to mimic his movements and follow his exact footsteps. The air around us was dark and confining. It was almost heavy as it pressed into us on all sides. James slowed his pace and reached a hand back toward me. I touched it briefly to let him know I saw it and turned my head back to Damien to whisper, "James stopped."

We stood huddled together and James pointed up ahead at a strange shimmering effect on the leaves in the near distance.

"What is it?" Damien asked.

"I'm not sure," James replied. "I think it's only the sun. We must be approaching a clearing."

"Thank goodness," I exhaled.

"Follow me," James said, and started walking toward the shimmer. As the minutes passed, the air got lighter and brighter until we suddenly broke through into the clearing. I shaded my eyes, almost giddy from relief. I could breathe again. Once my eyes adjusted to the bright sunlight, my jaw dropped in amazement. We were in a kind of meadow. There were trees and shrubbery but mostly there were wildflowers. Wildflowers unlike anything I had ever seen or imagined. Red, orange, and yellow blossoms grew along dark, twisting vines along almost every rock and tree. The flowers almost looked like they were on fire. The petals were wispy and fluid as they fluttered in the breeze.

Damien brushed past me and took a deep breath of air. He looked as relieved as I felt to be out of the dark confinement of the trees. I don't think he even saw the flowers, he was so anxious to keep moving.

"Let's continue," he called back as he walked ahead of us. He moved quickly and James and I soon fell a little behind. I felt almost intoxicated by the strange beauty around me. We both leaned over to examine a brilliant red blossom blooming in the middle of thick, dark green coils. They wove intricately around a dark tree trunk with flowers scattered throughout the entire design.

"What are these?" I asked incredulously.

"I've never seen anything like them." James answered, equally enthralled.

I leaned closer to smell the alluring petals when James suddenly placed a hand on my shoulder, impeding my movement.

"Careful, Claire," he warned. "We don't know what these plants might do."

I rolled my eyes. "They're just flowers and I wasn't going to eat it or anything," I laughed as I looked over at him. I hadn't realized how close we were and when I turned my head our noses were only a few inches apart. We looked at each other for a few seconds before simultaneously pulling away awkwardly.

"Two more," James blurted out.

"What?" I asked. I had no idea what he was talking about.

"You have two more freckles on your nose."

I was silent.

"I just thought you might want to know," James smiled.

I burst out laughing. Awkwardness dispelled, we fell easily into step a few feet apart.

I glanced over at him and smiled. "I'm *so* glad you're keeping track for me."

"Don't mention it," he said.

"No, that's what I would prefer that *you* do. Don't mention them."

James chuckled.

"I hardly need reminding that I no longer have flawless skin," I said ruefully.

"And who said freckles are flaws?" he retorted.

"Oh yes, I forgot," I smiled. "Your sister has freckles and you like them."

"Besides," James continued as if I hadn't spoken. "I think you looked a little funny without them."

"What?" I gasped and nearly stumbled. I was genuinely stunned.

"I'm sorry," James laughed at my reaction. "I thought you looked a little pale or something. It was unnatural."

"Well, you were very mistaken then," I huffed. "I have it on unimpeachable authority that my cheeks had the perfect sheen of rosiness and health to compliment the peach of my skin tone."

James laughed again and held up his hands in surrender. "It's just my opinion," he said.

I scowled at him. No one had ever found my perfect appearance wanting before. I didn't like it. He had once called my gifts my "consolation prize," and although I had indignantly protested, I feared that he might have been right, at least to some degree. Now I was annoyed at his insult *and* annoyed that he had been correct. How irritating. I quickened my pace and brushed past him haughtily. In my haste, and with my newfound clumsiness, I accidentally bumped into a tangle of vines and disrupted a flower's peaceful state of gentle fluttering. I caught my balance before James could reach out and steady me. James rolled his eyes, as usual.

"What?" I asked, pretending I didn't realize how petty I was being.

A strange noise interrupted whatever reply he was about to make. It was like a crackle or snapping sound. I looked around in confusion. James did the same and then suddenly grabbed my arms and pulled me to him. He spun me around and began stamping his foot around the ground by my ankles.

"What are you doing?" I yelled, confused and still annoyed.

Smoke wafted up to my nose and I looked behind me at where he had stamped on my gown. The fabric was torn and blackened by fire. I was still in James's arms and I twisted back around to face him. He looked as confused as I felt. He opened his mouth to speak, but I held up my hands and attempted a joking remark to diffuse the unease that now seemed to grip both of us.

"Yes, yes, I know. That's what you're here for." My efforts were rewarded with a somewhat puzzled smile.

"Where did that come from?" he asked.

"I have no idea," I responded. He let me go and examined the back of my gown to make sure the fire was completely put out. I then heard the crackling noise again and jumped back, away from the sound. We both looked down at the flower I had bumped. My head tipped to the side in kind of horrified wonder as we saw tiny sparks of fire coming from the center and tips of the petals.

CHAPTER SEVENTEEN

*T*he sparks continued and grew larger and the air picked up speed. Gusts of air plowed through the trees, upsetting each flower, causing them each to bloom, snapping and sparking. Soon, the crackle of fire and the noise from the wind was deafening. James and I were speechless as we stared around us at what should have been impossible. The wind carried the sparks of fire around and around, creating little tunnels and rings. I watched in horror as each ring grew larger and larger. The wind was creating whirlwinds of fire. James grabbed my hand shouting, "Run!" as he dragged me out of the way of a small cyclone nearly as tall as I was. We ran as the tornados grew larger and larger, sucking in entire trees, which then erupted into flame, fueling the fire and making them even larger. I screamed as a flaming trunk crashed down in front of me. The intensity of the heat took my breath away and my eyes watered. James jerked me toward him just before a smoking rock plummeted toward me. We spotted Damien several paces ahead sprinting for a large boulder. We ran after him. James shoved me around the back of the huge rock beside Damien and threw his weight over me as the wind grew stronger and more insistent. We huddled close, clinging to the rock with all the strength we could muster. The rock began to shudder and tremble from the strain of the gusts of wind. I opened my eyes and looked up at James, who was trying to shout something to

Damien and me, but I couldn't hear anything over the clamoring din around us. James jerked his head to his left and I shifted my head to try and see what he was gesturing at. I could barely see through the smoke and debris flying around us, but I thought I could make out a small ravine or ditch. James tried to pull us away from the rock when we were still unable to hear what he was shouting, but Damien and I resisted. The idea of leaving our only source of shelter seemed ludicrous. Then, the boulder started shaking and I knew it was moments away from being torn into the middle of the fiery whirlwind and us along with it. I threw myself at James and the three of us ran toward the ditch. The force of the wind made me feel like I was running into a brick wall. I felt myself being violently pulled back. My feet slipped and I screamed soundlessly in the blaring uproar. James grabbed me around my waist and yanked my body back toward him, hauling me along with him as he dug each foot into the ground and plowed his way through the wind. Damien had reached the ditch and disappeared over the edge. James threw me down next to Damien and then landed on top of me. I shut my eyes tightly and focused on the feeling of rough dirt, weeds, and stones on my cheeks and chest and under my arms. The weight of Damien to the side and James pressing down on my back compressed my lungs and I strained to keep breathing. Tears escaped my tightly shut eyes and mingled with the soil beneath my face, which then stuck to my cheeks and crept into my nostrils. Although I could tell James was trying to cover me from the elements, I felt like I was suffocating. I fought to keep calm and to keep my breathing slow and even. After what seemed like an eternity, I noticed that the winds were slowly quieting. The soft sounds of moaning and choking startled me when I realized it was the sound of my sobs. The noise continued to dissipate until I could only hear the three of us panting heavily. James stirred and he ventured a look around.

"Aurora," Damien said, gingerly moving my shoulders and trying to turn me around.

"Are you alright?" James asked, concern coloring his voice.

I drew in a deep, trembling breath, pushed up on my palms, and forced myself into a kneeling position. I then carefully sat back on my heels and ran my hands over my forehead and face, feeling for any damage. I felt dirty, but in one piece. My ribs were bruised and my lungs ached from constriction and smoke inhalation. I looked up at James and Damien. Their faces were smudged with dirt and ash and their hair stuck out at all angles. James's clothes were torn along his back. I could see that he had absorbed most of the shock. Tears filled my eyes again and started running down my cheeks.

"What's wrong?" James asked quickly.

"Are you hurt?" Damien demanded worriedly.

"No, no," I waved them away. "I mean, I suppose I'm a little bruised and scratched, but I feel awful," I sobbed.

"Where?" James asked, examining my limbs, checking for breaks or fractures in my bones.

"No, I just feel awful that this whole thing was my fault," I moaned, pulling my wrist away from James.

Damien looked surprised.

"How was this your fault?"

I gulped and said, "I was walking and—"

"And I accidentally bumped into her and we nudged one of those fire flowers," James interrupted me. I looked over at him in surprise and started to protest but he put a gentle pressure on my arm to silence me.

"You idiot!" Damien raged. "You could have killed us all with your clumsy stupidity."

"No, he—" I was interrupted again, this time by Damien.

"You're sure you're alright, darling?" he asked me.

"Yes, but—"

"Alright then; I'm going to find a stream or something where we can wash up." And with that he was up and moving away from us.

"Why did you do that?" I reproached James.

"Do what?" he asked innocently as he slowly stood up, examining the tears in his sleeve and tunic.

"Take the blame for me. You know Damien wouldn't have reproached me the way he did you."

"Well, it was my fault. I provoked you and made you lose your balance because you were angry with me," James insisted.

"Don't be stupid," I said, annoyed that he was being so gallant when I had been so awful. "You know I was being ridiculous and had no right to get angry with you."

"Well, I did insult your pale complexion." He tried for a smile. "Although you certainly have enough color now."

My hands flew to my face and I felt the crusted dirt covering almost my entire face. I assumed that my tears had paved little streaks down my cheeks and I recalled mud filling my nostrils. I cringed at how I must look. James let out a small laugh and then winced.

"Are you alright?" I asked, ashamed that I hadn't thought to ask before. I was at the bottom of the pile, after all.

"I'm fine," James assured. "Just a little sore."

I nodded. Then my breath hitched like a little girl who had been crying too hard and I blushed, under all the mud.

"Thank you for saving me," I said quietly. "And for taking the blame."

"Claire, even if you had purposefully hit a flower or even picked one, there is no way you could have guessed what would happen," James said kindly. "How could any of us have known? It's not anyone's fault."

"Well, I still learned my lesson," I said wearily, getting to my feet. "Until we're out of this forest, I'm not unnecessarily touching anything."

James and I walked in the direction Damien had gone. He was vigorously scrubbing his face and arms in a stream close by, his sleeves rolled up to his elbows. I started to hurry toward the water when James's voice cautioned me.

"Let me make sure this water is alright."

I glanced at Damien. He seemed fine. James crouched next to the water's edge and tentatively reached a hand in. He swirled the water around a bit, then smelled, and eventually tasted it. Finally he was satisfied and he gave me a nod.

I rushed forward, eager and yet hesitant to see my reflection and determine just how bad I really looked. But James again held me back and said quietly, "Maybe you should just rinse a little before you look."

I looked at him quizzically. "How did you know I was going to look at my reflection?"

"Let's just say I'm getting used to you." He smirked.

"That's very thoughtful of you to consider my reaction to my appearance, but you do realize that now I have to know because you've made me feel that I must look even worse than I imagined," I said with a somewhat embarrassed smile.

"Have it your way." James threw up his hands in the air and walked back over to the water's edge. I separated myself by a stone's throw down the stream and then peered at myself in the clear water. Damien and James both jumped in surprise when I let out a horrified shriek. I had never looked so hideous in my life. Up until a few weeks ago I was incapable of even looking remotely hideous, but this was just absurd. My hair was one hugely disheveled disaster, my face was covered with gravel and dirt with bits of weed sprouting out and the few bits of skin not encased with mud were smeared with black ash and soot. Little streaks ran from my eyes and nose down to my chin. And my dress was completely ruined.

"My face looks like a field that's been trampled by a dozen horses," I moaned dejectedly.

I heard James chuckle and Damien called back, "Don't worry, darling. I still find you as irresistible as ever." I heard the mocking laughter in his voice, but it still warmed my heart to hear it. He had been so distant lately and his derision was reassuring somehow.

A few moments later I heard Damien sigh in frustration. "This is impossible," he groaned. "I'm going to find a spot for a more thorough wash. Keep an eye on Claire for me, will you?" he asked James as he trudged through some bushes to a more private bathing area.

I did my best to scrub my face and arms clean and then meandered back over to James. He had removed his tunic, and his white shirt was wet from his washing. I noticed a growing red stain on James's sleeve, just below his left shoulder.

"James," I cried out. "What happened to your arm?"

He looked surprised at my outburst.

"Oh, it's nothing. A rock or something skimmed my arm as it flew by. It's just a scratch," he assured me.

I was not convinced and demanded that I see it.

"Honestly, the water made the blood spread and it looks worse than it is," he said, pulling up his sleeve gingerly.

It wasn't as bad as I feared from the amount of red on his sleeve, but it didn't look like a tiny scratch either.

"Hold still and don't look for a second," I commanded. He dutifully sat on a rock while he made an exaggerated display of covering his eyes with his forearm. The boyishness of this gesture suddenly made my heart feel like I was snuggled up in front of a cozy fireplace. I shook myself thoroughly and ducked behind him. I turned around and tore off a piece of one of my petticoats, one of the few layers of me that wasn't filthy. Armed with a bandage, I advanced on James, taking his arm in my hands and wrapping the linen securely around the cut several times and securing it with a tight knot. Feeling a little strange for a moment, I finished tying the knot and my hands still rested on his arm. This was the first time I'd ever really seen a man's arm . . . this close to the shoulder, at least. I wondered if all arms were so large and muscular and then blushed at my girlish stupidity. Of course, I had no right or reason to concern myself with James's arms, no matter how strong. James seemed to be ignoring me entirely and focusing on the swirling water in front of him. He couldn't have any notion of my thoughts, but I felt shy and awkward nonetheless and made a joke to cover my embarrassment.

"I feel like the heroine of a book or something. Here I am bandaging wounds with scraps of my clothing."

James gave a tight laugh and continued looking straight ahead.

I drew back and cleared my throat. "Well, there you go. You're good as new," I said brightly. Actually, I had no idea. I had no training in anything medicinal or anything really practical at all, but the bandage looked secure and I supposed it was better than letting him bleed to death.

"Thank you, Your Highness," James said with a gallant bow.

I just nodded.

"Well, I think I'll go wash up a bit more as well," I said, backing away. "I won't go far. Just behind those trees there," I motioned.

"Alright," James said. "I'll be here if you need me."

"Thanks again," I said as I turned to go, wanting to hide my blushing face. Maybe there was something to be said for covering up with dirt if people couldn't see your flushed cheeks.

Once I was modestly hidden by a few trees, I carefully removed my clothing down to my undergarments and chemise. I tried my best to scrub my gown and petticoats and then laid them on a rock in the sun to dry a little. I finger combed my tangled hair and rubbed my arms and legs as the soft breeze caused my skin to prickle with goose bumps. I reached over for my gown. It was still damp, but no longer dripping wet. I threw my gown back over my head and pulled it into place. I decided to leave the petticoats. Their weight only dragged me down now and the ends were hopelessly frayed. The lower portions of my sleeves were also in a horrible state so I tore them off, letting the tight heavy muslin stop at my elbow. My hair felt heavy as I lifted it over my shoulder and continued to squeeze water out of it. I finger combed through it as best as I could, but I didn't know what on earth I was supposed to do with it. My hairnet had been lost in the firestorm and I had no idea how to braid my own hair. I tried twisting it this way and that to no avail. I was stuck with thick damp hair that went nearly to my waist. Eventually, I emerged from my thicket of privacy and found James much as I had left him, only cleaner. I cleared my throat and he looked over expectantly.

"Yes?" he asked.

"Um," I felt terribly awkward. "My hair . . ."

James's shoulders drooped as he started to roll his eyes again.

"Claire, I did my best to protect us and our belongings, but I can't be held responsible for the state of your hair—"

"No, no," I rushed to explain. "I'm so grateful. You know that. I just . . . It's just that I—I don't know what to do with it."

James's head tilted a bit in confusion.

"I mean, I can't just leave it like this. It's too heavy. It will get in the way."

A glimmer of understanding flickered in his face.

"Can't you just braid it?" he asked with a shrug, probably wondering why I had added yet another thing for him to worry about.

"Please don't laugh at me, or think me even sillier than I know you already do, but. . . . Well, the fact of the matter is . . . I don't know how." I hung my head in shame.

After a moment's silence I heard a loud peal of laughter and looked up to find James shaking with mirth.

"I asked you not to laugh," I grumbled.

"I'm sorry, Claire," he said through laughter. "I just didn't even think that was possible. Don't all girls know how to do that sort of thing? Don't you practice on each other?"

I fumed at his male naivety. "All girls don't—"

"Don't fall asleep for a hundred years, I know. You really need to let that go."

I gaped at him in response.

"Are you really making light of the fact that I lived with that hanging over my head?" I asked in shock.

"No, I'm not trying to. But you're alive right now. You're living now. You're doing something important and making judgment calls that you've never had to make. And you're doing a good job," he finished with a kind look that stopped me in my tracks.

"Well, I— thank you," I stuttered.

"You're welcome. Now, back to the matter at hand. Why don't you know how to braid hair? I actually can't believe I'm even talking about this."

"Okay, okay, I get it. It's not big deal to you, but I really don't know how to do anything with my hair other than stuff it into a net, which was lost in the storm. My attendants have always done my hair, not to mention, my hair mostly did what they told it to without much prodding at all. And as for braiding each others' hair, I'll remind you that I never really had any friends, so there's that." I finished my speech in embarrassment and I looked at my hands. James seemed to realize the time for teasing was over.

"Well, I could braid it for you," he offered softly.

My head snapped up and I saw genuine concern and feeling on his face for my plight, which was very kind, but I just couldn't get past the fact that James knew how to braid hair. How? How was that even possible?

"*You* know how to braid *hair*?" I asked in amazement, my jaw dropping nearly to the forest floor. At that moment, James seemed to realize what he had admitted to and held up his hand.

"I'm asking you to let this go," he warned. A mental picture of this tall, hulking man braiding hair in his large hands threatened to undo me and I felt a giggle rising in my chest. He recognized my mirth and grimaced in an attempt to look menacing.

"Don't you dare laugh," he growled. My laughter burst out of me in an extremely undignified crow-like noise that ended with me snorting and hiccupping at the same time. I suppose he found that amusing enough that he forgot his annoyance and he joined me until we were both gasping for air between bouts of laughter. I slowly calmed myself as I noticed with pleasure how young and carefree James looked when he laughed. He even had a hint of a dimple on his left cheek.

After taking a deep breath, I began again.

"So, tell me, how did you acquire such a skill?"

He moaned and shook his head as he finally stopped laughing.

"If you must know, I have a sister. She made me help her with her hair while we were growing up."

"Oh yes, the one with freckles?" I smiled. A female version of James? What would that even look like?

"Yes. And if you promise not to tease me about it, I will braid your hair and teach you how to do it yourself."

I smiled in agreement and came closer to him, sitting on the rock to his right. He raised a finger and twirled it exaggeratedly so I would turn around and face the opposite direction. I hastily obeyed.

"Alright, the trick with braiding is make the sections even," he began, as he picked up my hair and started separating it.

"How many sections?" I asked.

"Three."

I felt him moving the pieces and his hands brushed my back a few times, which made me shiver even though I tried not to.

"Sorry, I must still be a little cold from washing up," I quickly apologized when I realized his hands had stilled. He didn't move for another moment and I asked, "Is everything okay back there?"

He quickly cleared his throat and his hands started moving my hair again.

"Yes, you just have a lot of hair. And you need to stop moving." He sounded a bit gruff.

"Fine, but you need to tell me what you're doing or how else will I figure out how to do this on my own? I can't very well ask you to do this every morning, can I?" His hands stilled again and I imagined him rolling his eyes in exasperation. I turned my head and was surprised to find his cheeks red.

"Or can I?" I teased, wiggling my brows.

"I draw the line at being a lady's maid, Your Highness," he pretended to scowl and then brought the braid around so that it was in front of me and he could show me how the three pieces wove together. It seemed simple enough.

"Alright, I think I can do that," I mused.

"Well, I should hope so, it's not exactly complicated," he said dryly.

"Must not be if you could learn," I quipped.

He looked up at me and tweaked my nose. "Watch your tone, Sass, or you're on your own."

I smiled and took my hair from his hands, pulling it all over my shoulder so it was in front of me.

"Let's see, you put this one over and then this side . . ."

"That's right," James encouraged.

"But I'm worrying about starting it," I said as I focused on my hair. "I wish there was someone I could practice on." I turned my face up to look at him, or more specifically, his hair. Unfortunately it was much too short.

James backed away as though afraid for his life.

"Stay away from me," he laughed. "Damien's hair is longer than mine. Try him."

I chuckled as I fastened the end of the braid with a string from my pocket.

"Didn't that gown used to be green?" Damien teased as he approached.

I smiled as I looked down at the color, which now appeared to be more of a mossy brown.

"I was tired of that color anyway," I retorted.

James finished up securing the bedrolls and food sacks on his back.

"How were you able to save our things?" I asked incredulously.

"I threw them down with you in the ditch. Our weight protected them, thankfully."

"Unfortunately, one of the bundles was ripped away before we reached it," Damien said looking around for the missing sack, sounding a little annoyed. "I'm afraid you and I will have to make do with only one change of clothing."

"Oh, that's fine," I assured them. "I'm grateful you were able to save anything at all."

James smiled at me in response. "That's what I'm here for." His voice was weary, but attempting humor. And I grinned at our inside joke.

"So where to now?" I asked.

"We'll continue north until dark and make camp. We just have to keep going until we reach the heart of the forest, which I'm told is near a lake or something similar." James outlined the plan as he picked up a large branch to use as a walking stick.

We set off, Damien and I following James at a brisk pace. Hours later we finally stopped as the sun began to fall slowly below the horizon. He had only one small tent, which I received gratefully. I gobbled up a few dried fruits and pieces of smoked meat before falling to my bedroll in exhaustion.

I stared out the window as the clouds steadily darkened. I could see the leaves moving ferociously as the wind whipped the branches back and forth, almost violently. I tried not to flinch too noticeably when the lightning struck and the thunder boomed, but I felt the shudder down to my core. At eleven years old, I was determined to show my fearlessness in the face of storms. After all, I already knew my fate. How could a storm

hurt me? That reasoning kept my fear of most things at bay, but for some reason my fear of these wretched storms had stayed with me from my youngest years.

I knew Angeline and my mother loved these storms. I could see how they were thrilling, but that flash of whitish purple and the horrible accompanying boom and crackle made my breathing quicken and my pulse speed up.

A particularly loud rumble startled me so badly I dropped my book on my foot and winced at the pain. I turned quickly from the window and fled to the safety of my canopy bed and soft covers.

CHAPTER EIGHTEEN

I awoke with what seemed like a flash of lightning and then blinked my eyes rapidly, trying to crawl out of my dreams. I rubbed my face and mumbled a good morning to Damien and James and wandered over to the stream for some refreshment. After splashing my face and finally forcing my hair into a tangled braid after three frustrating attempts, I walked back to camp. Damien nodded at me absently as he walked toward the stream himself.

"Nice braid," James teased and tugged on my hair as he walked past with the bedrolls.

"You would know," I shot back with a smile.

He smirked and continued toward the horses.

After a hurried breakfast—I couldn't remember the last time I had eaten a leisurely meal—we made an early start and began walking. Compared to our adventure the previous day, it seemed quite uneventful. We walked for hours before stopping briefly to rest and eat a little at midday. After our short break we continued onward. The scenery around me seemed to blur into one endless row of trees and shrubbery. The ground was soft and muddy in most areas and it made the strain on my muscles all the worse. At one point I realized I was falling a little behind the men and I told my tired legs to move faster as I hurried after them. I tripped on my way over to Damien and I flailed my arms wildly as I struggled to regain my footing in the mud. I lurched over to Damien and grabbed onto his arm to keep myself from pitching face forward into the dirt. Damien looked annoyed and I flushed.

"I'm sorry," I apologized. "I'm sure this clumsiness will wear off."

"It's fine, darling." It didn't sound fine. He looked down at his pants and futilely tried to brush off the rather large spatters of mud that I'd caused.

"I'm going to go rinse these off," he said as he walked off in the direction of the stream.

"I guess that means we're taking our supper now," James muttered as he loosened a knapsack from his shoulder and started pulling out some dried meats and fruits.

I shrugged miserably and looked up at the sky. The sun was nowhere near setting. It was at least an hour before we normally stopped for food, but James was right. Who knows how long Damien would be and there was no sense making two long stops before making camp for the night. I noticed James watching me and I looked over at him.

"I know, I know," I mumbled. "If I wasn't so clumsy, we wouldn't be wasting this time."

"That's not what I was thinking," James answered and handed me an apple.

"What were you thinking?" I asked, taking a bite and self-consciously wiping a bit of juice as it rolled down my chin.

"I was wondering if Damien really intends to keep his clothes clean for this entire journey."

I saw him smile and I couldn't help but give a little chuckle.

"He appreciates cleanliness, I suppose," I offered lamely. James nodded, doing his best to keep a straight face.

"Well, there are worse things, aren't there?" I swatted at his arm. He easily dodged my hand and nodded again.

"Eat your food, sir," I commanded, pretending annoyance.

"Yes, Your Highness," he said over a mouthful of apple.

I smiled at him and took a seat on a log. After a moment's hesitation, he joined me, sitting an arm's length away. I enjoyed our companionable silence as we chewed our meats. I glanced over at him again and noticed that it was a little harder to make out his features. It was suddenly darker than it had been before. I looked up at the sky. Dark clouds had moved in and the sun was merely a dim light behind them. I looked over at James who seemed equally surprised.

"Those clouds rolled in fast," I remarked, feeling rather fidgety.

"A little too fast," he agreed as he scrutinized the sky above us.

"Do you think a storm is—" I was interrupted by a blinding flash of light. I blinked rapidly trying to adjust my vision. Before I could gain my bearings, a clap of thunder shook the air around us. I felt the deep shudder down to my bones. After my dream during the night before this was bringing unpleasant memories. James jumped up and reached for my hand to pull me up next to him.

"We need to move," he said, retying and strapping his bags. "By the sound of it, that lightning is close. We don't want to be near these trees." I nodded numbly and followed close behind. Suddenly the lightning flashed again and I threw up my hands to shield my eyes from the bright light. My breathing was starting to come in sharp, heaving gasps now and I noticed everything looked purple for a moment before going dark again. The thunder came a few seconds later as the ground trembled beneath us, and James pulled me away from the cluster of trees where we were. Another flash followed dangerously close to the last and the rumbling was almost instantaneous with the bright purple blaze. A jagged vein of lightning streaked down the sky and landed not far off in the distance and a large tree erupted in white flames before suddenly disappearing.

"What's happening?" I yelled to James. If he heard me in the deafening roar of thunder he made no sign. His only response was to move more quickly, dragging me along by the hand. I didn't know where we were headed, but his strides were purposeful so I trusted he had a plan.

Then the lightning struck closer. A tree only a few feet away shook with the purple spark and it too burst into flames before disappearing. I screamed in terror as I realized that it had fallen straight down into the earth. A smoking hole stood where the tree had once been. I grabbed James's arm and pointed. He nodded grimly and pulled me back into a jog. The breaks between thunderclaps grew shorter until there was almost no space between them. Lightning struck all around us, creating gaping cavities in the earth that smoldered with white, crackling smoke. We started sprinting. Garish, purple streaks shot down around us like rain. The air was bright white with a light, unearthly purplish glow. The thunder shook the ground and I struggled to keep my footing, but James ran on, dodging holes and avoiding the sinking strikes.

Lightning struck everywhere. My eyes ached from the brightness and the heat. Then, a sudden burst of hot wind, thunder, and blinding light knocked me off my feet. I flew through the air, trying wildly to grasp onto something. I landed painfully on my side; my ears rang and I couldn't see. The ground beneath me crumbled and I started to fall. I screamed out as I felt the earth give way. A hand suddenly grasped mine and I hung suspended in the air. I couldn't see my rescuer. I could only see bright splotches of purple and white.

"Don't let go!" I begged, but I couldn't hear myself. I tried screaming louder, but everything was muffled. I could only hear a loud and incessant ringing.

The hand pulled my arm little by little. I felt my body rising and gradually brought over a sort of ledge. Strong arms enfolded me for a moment before hauling me up to my feet. My legs instantly buckled and I screamed as I started to fall again. I felt James lift me up and toss me over his shoulder and I cried out as my bruised ribs came in sharp contact with his shoulder. We were moving again. Every step jarred me and I bit my lip to keep from crying. I still couldn't see or hear anything, but I felt the tremors shaking the air and earth. James maneuvered through the treacherous space, dodging here, leaping there. I suddenly felt him jump forward and we landed in a tangled heap. I struggled to sit up, to keep going. We couldn't stay still. We had to keep moving. I felt James restrain my movements. I continued to resist until he pushed my hands to my sides and held them there in a vice like grip. I couldn't move. I struggled to calm my breathing. The ringing in my ear was starting to lessen. I thought I could hear James telling me something.

"What?" I shouted. "I can't hear you! I can't see anything!"

I couldn't see anything. The realization that I was blind set in and I started writhing again. My back arched and I threw my head back in panic. I thought I heard James shouting my name. I ignored him. I couldn't see. I felt the tears falling down my cheeks and I continued to fight the arms that tried to restrain me. If I didn't get out of this grip I thought I might suffocate. My breathing became sharper and more and more shallow. My head felt faint as I realized I wasn't getting any oxygen. My panic increased and I strained to even breathe at all. The arms released me and I felt alone for a split second. Then two hands cupped my face. I thought I felt a forehead pressed to mine and a nose that brushed my nose. I tried to shake my head, but the hands held me firm. I felt something else then. An anxious, gentle pressure on my cheeks and face. It was too soft to be hands and it felt warm and smooth. The little touches moved about my face and I felt warm breath wisp around my ears and on my forehead. It distracted me and I felt my lungs fill with air. I reached out and clung to the arms. James's arms. I fought to regain control. I forced myself to calm my breathing and not faint. I forced myself to stop struggling. I focused on the faint sound of James's voice breaking through the thick fog in my head. I was regaining my hearing. Maybe I would regain my sight as well. I felt a tear roll down my cheek as I shook with repressed movement.

"Claire!" James yelled. I could barely hear him.

"Y-yes?" I stammered.

"Can you hear me?" he asked frantically.

"Yes, barely," I answered.

He gave a huge sigh of relief, pulling me toward him in a frenzied hug. "Stay calm. You'll be alright."

"I-I can't see," I bit back a few tears.

"Your vision will return just like your hearing," he assured me. "Just calm down. Be patient."

"How do you know?" I demanded. His moment's hesitation terrified me and I started struggling again.

"Claire, stop moving," his voice was rough, trying to get through to me. He pulled me toward him and rubbed my temples, gently massaging the area around my eyes. I took deep breaths.

"Was I hit by lightning?" I asked.

"Almost," James answered. "It hit directly in front of you."

"Why weren't you affected?"

"I was turned in the opposite direction so my hearing was momentarily stunned, but not my sight."

"And then I fell," I shuddered.

"After it threw you, you landed almost inside of a hole from a previous hit. I caught you before you disappeared."

"Thank you," I whispered. "You're always saving me."

"That's what I'm here—" he tried to laugh as he gave his standard answer, but it got caught in his throat.

"Where are we?" I could hear the rumble of thunder, but it sounded muted somehow.

"A cave," he responded. "I spotted it in the distance as the storm started."

"Of course you did," I attempted to laugh. "You seem to be prepared for anything."

"How are your eyes?" he asked.

"I don't know. Before, I saw only bright light, but now it's dim, almost black. I'm trying not to think about it."

"Well, your eyes are closed."

"Oh, of course they are," I said, a little embarrassed.

"Try opening them," James suggested.

"I'm afraid to," I admitted.

"It's alright. Just try it. We have to wait out this storm anyway. We have lots of time."

I slowly lifted my eyelids. I saw a difference in light. It was subtly brighter, but not much. I thought I could make out hazy forms, but I wasn't sure.

"Everything looks blurry," I told James. "It's like I'm underwater."

"Can you see me?" he questioned.

"Not really," I answered. I tried to focus where his voice was coming from. Slowly a vague form began to take shape. I reached out to touch the round outline across from me.

"Is this your head?" I asked.

"Yes," his voice was encouraging. "You're getting it. Just relax and let your eyes adjust. They've had a tremendous shock."

"You're telling me," I said dryly. I felt his jaw move a bit and heard him chuckle before I brought my hands back to my lap.

"I just realized something," I started. "Why wasn't it raining? Shouldn't there have been some rain? And why was it so purple?"

"Who knows why anything is the way it is in this place?" James shrugged. "I'm just wondering what else can happen."

"Yes, well, I'd prefer *not* to think about that," I muttered. I tried focusing on his face again and found that I could make out dark spots where his eyes and mouth should be.

"I can see you a little more," I said with excitement.

"That's good," he smiled.

The thunder roared on at the opening of the cave and I shuddered.

James seemed to take it upon himself to distract me. He took one of my hands in his much larger one. It was a sweet gesture that felt both brotherly and not at all brotherly at the same time.

He appeared to be trying to think of something to say that would take my mind off of the storm raging close by.

"So, from what I've gathered, you were told your story a lot growing up, true?" he asked.

"Yes," I hedged.

"Did they ever tell you why?" James continued.

"Why what?" I was puzzled.

"Why it all happened."

"You mean, why she—cursed me?" I clarified.

"Yes," James sounded careful, not sure how sensitive the topic was. I was quiet for a full minute before he started to say, "You don't have to talk about—"

"Her name was Zora," I blurted out. I felt him sort of nod in a gesture that I should continue.

"She was queen of the Dark Faeries," I began.

"Dark Faeries?"

"Yes, they live past the Northern Mountains. They practice dark magic and are notoriously volatile," I explained. He nodded again.

"Anyway, Zora had been their queen for quite some time. She was known as being powerful, sinister, and fiercely vindictive. Apparently she propositioned my father with some sort of alliance that involved, well, infidelity and a great deal of intrigue besides," I stammered through the awkward bits of the story. I had never had to tell it before. It felt strange. At his understanding silence, I continued.

"I understand that she made many similar arrangements with other kingdoms. Well, I don't know if you've met my parents, but they're very much in love." I heard him chuckle. "And principled as well. So my father turned her down emphatically and banned her from our kingdom. She was livid. And after I was born, Zora stormed into my fairy gifting ceremony and declared that I would die after pricking my finger on the needle of a spinning wheel at the age of sixteen. It was only because of Bernadette that I'm still alive today. She was the seventh fairy in the council and the only one that hadn't given me my gift yet. Most children don't receive fairy gifts. Fairies are temperamental, even the good ones. It's hard to convince them to do anything. Babies of the nobility will sometimes get one gift or maybe even two if they're lucky. But the council was so pleased with my father's outright refusal of Zora and her methods that they all came and I was given an unprecedented seven gifts."

"Ah, yes. The infamous fairy gifts of which you are so fond," James interrupted again, shaking his head, but I heard the smile in his voice.

"Yes, those," I said primly. Then my face darkened. "I think my parents blame themselves for the curse because of their fight with Zora. But of course it wasn't their fault. If I hadn't been born and if there hadn't been a gifting ceremony, none of this would have happened. So you see, I'm as much to blame, if not more so, than anyone else."

James shook his head vehemently and started to protest, but I quickly interrupted him.

"I know it sounds unreasonable to you," I persisted. "But that is the reality I have dealt with for a long time."

"But you can't just—" he tried again.

"It's alright," I assured him. "That's why you're here. That's why we're both here. We're figuring this mess out, once and for all." And before he could say anything else, I closed my eyes and leaned back against the smooth rock wall of our cave.

"I'm exhausted," I admitted.

"Why don't you rest your eyes for a minute?" James suggested after a few moments.

I covered another yawn with my hand.

I didn't think it possible to sleep in this situation, but I didn't want to talk anymore. So I kept my eyes shut and listened to the muffled crashes and explosions outside.

"Aurora!"

My eyes flew open and I winced at the dim light. But at least I could see! I looked around me, disoriented. I realized my head was on James's shoulder and his arm was wrapped around my waist. His cheek rested on my head and I could feel his breathing deep and steady. We had both fallen asleep. What had awakened me? I heard a scraping sound near the entrance of the cave and I felt James's body go suddenly rigid. I looked up at him and he seemed embarrassed by our proximity. I pulled away and turned toward the opening to see Damien's shocked face.

My jaw dropped. Where had he been all this time? More importantly, why, oh why hadn't this concerned me for even one moment before now? What on earth was wrong with me? I hadn't seen Damien in hours. He could have been killed in that storm. How could I not have even given him a thought?

"What is going on?" Damien's voice was frigid.

I quickly stood, followed promptly by James. The top of my head just barely touched the ceiling of the cave and the two men, especially James, had to hunch way over.

"Um, I was so worried about you," I said, stepping over to him.

"Why? And why were you two in this cave?"

143

"Why do you think?" I cried out. "We were escaping the lightning of course!"

"What lightning?" Damien demanded.

"What lightning?" I echoed, dumbly. How could he not have seen the lightning?

"Surely you saw it," James asked, as surprised as I was.

"I don't know what you're talking about," Damien snapped. "All I know is I went to stream and came back to find no one about. I've spent the last quarter of an hour searching for you."

"Damien," I started. "There was a storm. It was horrifying. There was lightning and thunder and white fire and holes in the earth. We're lucky to be alive!"

Damien looked very dubious.

"We'll show you," James led the way out of the cave.

My eyes watered at the brightness outside. I blinked rapidly until I could see more clearly and then I gasped in astonishment. There was no sign of gaping ditches, singed trees or any destruction whatsoever.

"What happened?" James breathed.

I looked around, trying to find some shred of evidence.

"Damien, this is crazy. Not only did a storm really happen, but it must be over an hour or two since you left for the stream and you say it's been how long?" I asked him.

"Under an hour, I'm positive," he responded. His face was fixed in a snarl.

"Wait," James beckoned us to follow him over to a small tree a few paces to our left. When we reached it, I saw one of the branches glitter and crackle giving off tiny sparks and puffs of white and purple smoke. Then, before our eyes, it calmed and any trace of fire disappeared.

"How is this possible?" I asked breathlessly.

"I don't know," James shook his head. "But I'm not waiting around to find out if this sort of thing happens in waves here. We've got to keep moving."

"Damien, you have to believe us. After the fire flowers, you know anything can happen in this awful forest," I persuaded.

"It's very strange," Damien said under his breath, but he fell into step beside me and we followed James quickly out of the clearing. Damien was moody and quiet for the rest of the day. I could hardly blame him. The day's events had been bizarre. There was no point trying to make sense of anything that happened here in this forest. Everything was upside down here. Topsy turvy. Like jagged, irregular pieces of a puzzle that didn't fit together. There was nothing to do but keep walking. We made camp quietly that night and we slept until morning.

CHAPTER NINETEEN

$\mathcal{I}$ placed my feet in the cool water the next morning and swirled them around a bit. I wiggled my toes and took another step so that the water came up above my ankles. I turned my head when I heard the sound of angry voices coming from back at camp.

"What now?" I muttered. It seemed that Damien and James were getting along less and less. The strain of the journey must have gotten to both of them. I sighed and pulled back my increasingly knotted hair into a braid, I noticed with satisfaction that I was getting better at that, and secured it with a ribbon. As usual, pieces fell forward, but as I checked my reflection in the water I saw that they did not naturally curl perfectly so as to accent each angle and curve of my face. Instead, they went off in several wispy directions, a few sticking to my still wet skin. I dried my cheeks and forehead with a handkerchief and did my best to smooth down my now stubborn hair. I also did my best to ignore the faint new freckle on my nose. I'd lost count of how many I now had. Seventeen? Maybe twenty. They were small and light, but they were most definitely there. I sighed and remembered what James had said about imperfections being part of what make people who they are. So maybe these new developments just made me more *me* . . . only a me that I had never realized was there before. Would they leave again once we figured out the cure for the relapse? Would I miss them? It was all very confusing.

I noticed that James's and Damien's voices had quieted and I realized I should be heading back to give them a chance to freshen up before we began the day's travels. I wiggled my toes again and gave a little splash for good measure before leaving the cool water and putting back on my stockings and boots.

I was walking back from the stream when I heard my name. I turned quickly to see Damien standing a few feet to my right, leaning against a tree. For some reason his presence surprised me. With James so friendly of late, and Damien so focused on our journey, I realized to my chagrin that I had been expecting James.

I smiled at him and walked over.

"What's going on?" I asked.

"Nothing, nothing at all," he said with a mischievous smile. He took both my hands in his and pulled me closer. "I guess I just wanted a few moments with you to myself," he cooed, bending down to kiss my cheek. I felt a little flutter of anxiety in my stomach. After the last few days with him mostly ignoring me, I felt more self-conscious and awkward than usual.

"Oh, well, that's nice," I stuttered. "We *have* been very busy, haven't we?" Before I could think of something wittier to say, Damien suddenly pulled me into his arms and kissed me.

I don't know what I felt. I think I was pleased, although a little shocked. He wound my arms around his neck before returning his arms to my waist and kissing me again. It lasted quite a long time and I was starting to feel a bit uncomfortable when some twigs snapped somewhere. Damien pulled away to look in the direction of the noise. I looked too, but didn't see anything out of the ordinary.

"What was that?" I whispered.

"Probably a rabbit," he murmured. He had a strange sort of triumphant gleam in his eye that I found odd, but dismissed it. He grabbed my hand and pulled me back to camp. My head whirled in confusion. Damien's emotions and mood changes were so hard to predict, not to mention keep up with. One minute he seemed to find me irresistible, and the next, I seemed to be no more than a mere presence at best, an irritant at worst. I thought back to how my hair looked and my new freckle and my face flushed hot. He probably found me hideous in this condition.

We reached camp still holding hands and I saw James pacing around the smoking embers. He looked up and then quickly away when we saw us.

"Oh, James," Damien said smoothly, "I thought you had gone to wash up."

James clenched his jaw and seemed a little tongue-tied. "No, I—I was waiting until she got back," he said with a jerk of his head in my direction.

"I told you I was collecting her. Sorry it took so long," he smiled. "We got a little . . . sidetracked."

I squirmed uncomfortably and looked at the ground.

"I'll go now then," James grunted and stalked off.

Damien squeezed my shoulder. "I guess I'll go wash up as well."

I was left alone while the two men went off to wash. I sat gingerly on a rock near what used to be a warm fire. A few of the embers still glowed a faint orange and I reached out to feel their lingering heat. I tried to make sense of Damien's and James's latest exchange. When they had first arrived at the castle I had thought them good friends. Now it seemed as though they could hardly stand each other. Damien was often flippant or patronizing toward James, who in turn seemed to do his best to ignore Damien. I closed my eyes and let my mind aimlessly wander. With a shock I realized I was trying to picture myself married to Damien and having a hard time doing so. And then it suddenly occurred to me that I might not actually want to spend my life married to such a temperamental husband. Not since my ninth birthday had I had such a rebellious thought. I had been told my story by the kingdom's greatest storyteller as I was told every year on my birthday. My parents thought that hearing the whole ordeal romanticized would make it easier on me. That was the first time I made the connection that the storyteller said that only I would be falling asleep. I burst out crying and ran to my mother and father begging to know if they would still be alive when I woke up. My mother had looked anxiously at my father and tried in vain to disguise the tears that sprang to her eyes.

"Now, now, my little Claire," my father had soothed, patting my golden curls. But he couldn't think of anything else to say. And so I had thrown my first real temper tantrum. My gifts of generosity and grace and gentility had kept my a very docile and sweet-tempered child, but the strength of my fear, sadness, and the crippling feeling of injustice had broken through and I raged. I raged on and on. I broke a few dishes, pulled my maid's hair, tore my dress, and stomped my little feet until they were bruised. I remember crying over and over, "I don't want to go to sleep" over and over until I was born away by several of my maids and nannies who eventually soothed me into a calmer state. That night, I snuck out of my room and wandered over to my parents' quarters. I heard my mother's muffled sobs and my father's agonized whispers of consolation. I peeked through the keyhole and saw my mother crying in my father's arms. I vowed then and there never to make my mother cry like that again. We couldn't change the spell, but I could at least act more cheerful about it and enjoy the time I had with them. From that time on I realized I had treated the curse as something romantic and exciting. I never complained. I never threw fits. I never let my parents see me cry. Occasionally at night in the privacy of my bedroom I would shed a few tears. For the most part, though, I believe I hid my emotions very well. I trained myself to accept things as they were. It was a bit of a habit now.

I stood up quickly and brushed my hands over my skirt. No more silly thoughts. No more rebelling. I needed to focus on the cause of the relapse. No use focusing on what couldn't be changed. No use focusing on what was out of my control. I would simply ignore it until I came to terms with it. I was good at that. Gifts or no, that was something I could do.

The men returned and James still avoided looking in my direction. He silently strapped and tied on our belongings and started walking. Damien and I followed. The mood was quiet and heavy for most of the day as we trudged on and on. Even lunch was a dreary affair. Finally, over a small hill we reached an immense expanse of land completely covered by enormous fallen tree trunks all lying at odd angles with deep crevices between them.

"What happened here?" I asked, puzzled.

James and Damien both shrugged, but the latter drew his sword and moved to push me behind him. At that, James moved even further away, refusing to even look in our direction. We approached the field of almost eerie stillness with apprehension and bewilderment.

The first tentative step I took onto one of the high tree logs was more of a stumble really. I used a gnarled knot as a foothold as I grasped the top and tried in vain to pull myself up. With a sigh of exasperation, James gave me a boost and then pulled me the rest of the way.

"What's the matter with you anyway?" I asked him, scowling.

"Nothing, Your Highness," he answered.

"Don't call me that, James," I frowned as I made an awkward leap to the next log, "You know what I'm talking about."

Damien's sudden proximity saved James from answering. Damien took my hand with firm pressure and led me carefully along while James proceeded to leap and bound until he was far ahead of us. I ignored the pang I felt and tried to focus on watching my own footing and Damien as he began speaking of our marriage celebration.

Just as Damien began to outline the geographical details of our post-wedding tour, I felt the ground shudder. The trunks quaked and I lost my balance a little, grabbing onto Damien for support.

"What was that?" I whispered.

Damien didn't answer but instead directed me to hold on to a branch before he jumped to the next log to yell after James who looked back at us, mirroring our perplexed expressions.

"Wait here," Damien instructed, going after James to consult with him what might be going on.

Well, perfect. Now I was alone. My trunk shivered again and I tried to quell my own shaking. I tried to regain a bit of my backbone. What were those defense techniques James had taught me? Oh bother. None of those would work with angry trees.

Half a minute had not gone by before the ground shook again with violent upheaval, only this time it didn't settle down. A deep rumble seemed to claw its way out of the ground. *Not again*, I thought with growing dread. Movement on my left made me jerk my head to look. Logs began to fly up at random moments almost as if they were alive and had a mind of their own. The rumbling increased to a deafening roar.

A huge trunk flew at my head. I bit off a scream and crouched down before it hurtled past, just making it over my trembling form. The logs looked as though they were rolling tumultuously down a steep ravine, but there was no decline here. We were on flat ground. I hid my face in my hands as I wrapped my arm more tightly around the branch.

Between my taut fingers I saw James and Damien as they jumped from trunk to trunk, trying to get to me, trying to avoid the crushing pressure of a furious blow. I saw a log come hurdling through the air toward James and I screamed in warning. He turned and ducked down just in time. His eyes locked on mine just as the log I clung to lurched violently and ripped the branch out of my hands. My back arched painfully as the log tossed me into the air. My scream sounded this time as my fingers clawed and grasped, reaching nothing, searching in vain for something to hold onto. I landed with an agonizing thud on another trunk. The breath left my lungs with violent force and I struggled in vain to fill my lungs with air. I tried to focus as stars raced across my consciousness. I looked up frantically and saw a massive tree plummeting toward me.

A strong arm suddenly wrapped around me, whisking me out of harm's way. A smaller branch whipped past me and caught me just under and slightly behind my ear. The pain shot through my head. My vision blurred and I felt my consciousness slipping. I looked up to find Damien's dazzling gray eyes staring into mine in what I can only describe as a frightened intensity. He held me tight in his arms, comforting me and dodging fatal blows. I glanced to my right and locked eyes with James who remained ahead, frozen on the jagged edge of a trunk. The roar slowly dimmed into a fuzzy buzz in my head, and James's tortured expression was the last thing I saw before I blacked out.

CHAPTER TWENTY

My head felt fuzzy and my limbs seemed too heavy to move. *No!* I thought in panic. This couldn't be it. I couldn't have fallen back under the curse before figuring out the cure. I struggled to open my eyes and gasped in relief when my eyelids fluttered and I saw the brightness of the sun above me. I also saw Damien and James. Their heads huddled over me in concern.

"How are you feeling?" Damien asked.

I groaned in response and gingerly reached to feel behind my ear. My fingers encountered a wad of cloth instead. James was pressing it securely to my head, the pressure hurt atrociously but I supposed it was better to stop the blood flow.

"When I saw that tree coming for you, I thought my life was over," Damien's voice cracked dramatically.

Strange that you left me in the first place then, I thought wryly before dismissing my annoyance. He couldn't have known what would happen. My headache was making me horribly irritable. I glanced at James to make some sort of joke about who was the doctor now, but the pain in his eyes shocked me into silence. He looked so angry and afraid and regretful I couldn't say anything. I looked away and after a few moments I managed to mutter, "I'm so tired of this cursed forest trying to kill us. How much longer until we reach the heart?"

"Not much longer now, I'm sure of it," Damien answered. "We'll camp here for the night and probably reach it by midday tomorrow." James was still silent as he held the compress to my wound.

"I can probably manage that now," I told him, putting my hand over his. He nodded once and removed his hand. I watched him set up camp from where I sat, still in Damien's arms, but he never looked up. Never met my eye.

The next morning dawned clear and shining. My head still ached a little but I was surprised at how refreshed I felt. The cut really wasn't very deep. Damien and James had probably made more of a fuss than was actually necessary. I dressed quickly. My blue gown was now almost as dirty as my green one. I emerged from my tent to find James putting out the fire and rolling up his and Damien's bedrolls.

"Damien is washing up," he said without a glance in my direction. "He'll be back soon."

"Thank you," I said glumly. I don't know what I had done to cause such a change in James. I felt the loss of his friendliness so keenly it surprised me. Unbidden, hot tears stung my eyes. I quickly dashed them away as I went back into my tent and folded my bedroll myself and then brought it out to James.

"Thanks," he nodded.

"James," I burst out. "Why—" I stopped, not knowing how to ask why he didn't like me anymore. How to ask what had happened to our friendship. James finally met my eyes, looking like it pained him intensely to do so. I swallowed and tried again.

"I just don't—" I was interrupted by Damien walking back into camp.

"Good morning," he flashed me a brilliant smile.

"Morning," I mumbled and walked over to the stream.

As we walked all morning I noticed the stream gradually getting a little wider and then a little louder and then a bit faster. James noticed this as well and informed us we should be getting to the lake very soon. Within an hour I saw the lake shimmering before us, the stream feeding into it ahead and to the left of where we were. We continued toward it until we reached an unusual looking sign. It almost looked like a grave marker.

THE GLASS LAKE.

That is what the engraving on the huge slab of granite near the path read. Nearby, a small white rowboat sat placidly in the cool green grass in coy invitation. I looked closer at the small warning etched below the title.

The Glass Lake is calm
It will lead you to what you seek
But a word of caution:
Sometimes Glass shatters

"Any ideas about what that is supposed to mean?" Damien asked, close to my shoulder.

His dark hair curled artistically over his ear and the beginnings of a beard grew on his strong face.

"None," I murmured as I took a step back, unsettled by his nearness. I glanced quickly at James. He stood on the shore, staring out across the mirror-like expanse.

It was certainly the largest lake I had ever seen. I could barely see the land on the horizon across from us. And the surface was seamless, utterly devoid of ripple or flaw.

"We're crossing it," Damien said.

"I'm not sure that's a good idea, Highness," James spoke quietly. "There's something strange about it. It's too smooth."

"We're going. The stone says it will lead us to what we seek. We have nothing else to go on." Damien's resolve was unflinching.

We pushed the white boat to the shore, and Damien placed himself at the front. James stuffed our belongings under a seat and reached out to help me into the boat behind Damien. I was surprised at how cold James's hand felt as he held mine to help me settle onto the narrow bench. He quickly released my hand. I turned away from

154

him moodily as he gave the boat the final push off and hopped into the back.

"I'll handle the oar," Damien insisted and dipped the oar in on each side of the boat, slicing the water like smooth butter on a breakfast table. I expected the oar to disturb the slippery stillness but nothing, not an ounce of unrest could be seen. The oar sliced in and out without disturbing a drop.

I stared at the water in puzzled fascination while Damien continued to make our way to the other side of the lake. I shouldn't have been surprised. Everything else we'd encountered in this place had been strange and unexpected, why not this?

When the novelty of the water's apparently magical properties had worn off, I stared at the back of Damien's glossy head. The quiet was making me nervous. I tried tapping my toe against the bottom of the boat but was immediately hushed by Damien. My pent up energy burst out, "How much longer, do you think?"

"Aurora!" Damien admonished sharply, "Will you please keep quiet?" His harsh tone stung my ears.

As if in response to the noise, the boat suddenly plunged downwards and a high-pitched cracking sounded. None of us had time to react before the boat lurched and heaved, completely out of control. My body jerked forward and slammed into Damien's back, which caused him to jolt forward as well, but he used the oar to steady himself. James quickly pulled me back and I clutched the sides of the boat, trying to right my position.

Frantic, Damien tried to establish some sort of secure hold with the oar. Water exploded over the sides, drenching us. I gulped for air as I groped for something to hold on to. Tall waves rose up and blasted into cutting droplets that stung in their fury as they pelted us relentlessly.

I cried out. The waves got larger and the boat less reliable. James pressed against my back, steadying me. I thought I heard him saying something, but the wind was too loud to be sure.

Wave after wave crashed against the boat. I gripped the sides with all the strength that I possessed just to keep from toppling over the edge. Damien tried to maneuver the oar to press forward, fighting the unpredictable waves with every stroke. James reached past me to grip Damien's shoulder.

"Give me the oar!" he shouted over the deafening chorus of crashing waves.

"I can do it," Damien insisted.

"You're exhausted!" James yelled, "Let me try."

Shards of prickly water nipped my face. The wind thrashed my wet hair against my back.

"Please, Damien," I cried. Waves threatened to tear the boat in pieces.

When he continued to ignore our pleas, James reached around me to grab the oar himself. In resistance, Damien lashed the oar back behind him and it connected sharply with James's head.

I screamed as his body went limp and he tumbled out the boat into the waves.

"Damien!" I shouted, "James is gone! He's in the water!" I frantically reached toward James's body, scrambling to pull him back to safety.

"What?" Damien yelled. I could barely hear him over the din of the storm.

A wave sucked James under and he was gone. No sign of him anywhere. I hysterically screamed his name over and over, then turned and started pounding on Damien's back for him to help James.

"Aurora!" Damien yelled back at me. For a moment he looked panicked. His eyes searched the water for James's body. He looked lost before shaking his head, clearing the water from his eyes. "He's a strong swimmer. He'll be alright." He kept nodding as though trying to convince himself.

"You can't know that!" I screamed. "You hit his head. He's not conscious." I continued to search the water with my eyes while I gripped the sides of the boat to keep from falling out.

"Aurora, we have to save ourselves now," Damien barked back at me, resolve gripping his expression.

I jerked away from him, shocked.

I turned back to look at the chaotic surface of the water surrounding the helpless boat, the place where James disappeared and my mind reached a sudden calm. In that moment I knew that my life would not be worth living without James in it.

I dove into the shattered depths of Glass Lake.

CHAPTER TWENTY-ONE

The water was so cold it snatched the air from my lungs. I gulped desperately for air only to fill my mouth with water. I fought, kicked, and clawed my way to the surface. I finally broke through and gasped for air. Coughing and sputtering, I couldn't see the boat anywhere. I couldn't see James either.

The water sucked me back under and my body was battered and tossed in every direction. My lungs burned. My fingers opened and closed as I fought to reach the surface again. I took in giant gulps of air before being sucked back under.

And then, through the crystal water I saw him. My mind somehow regained its calm and my body changed its course almost on its own. Determined strokes brought me to him. I clutched his shoulders. He was so heavy. My lungs threatened to explode as I fought again to break through to air. What had I been thinking? How could I get him to safety? How could I even save myself? I gripped him tighter and then suddenly felt us begin to move. I had no idea how, but the water seemed to help me drag him up toward the surface.

When we finally broke through I sucked in air with short, ragged breaths. James coughed and his eyelids fluttered once.

"James! Hold on. I've got you."

He didn't respond.

The water was suddenly calmer. I leaned back and tried to float while keeping hold of James's body. My eyelids flickered. I was so tired. But I could see the bank off in the distance. I could make it if I just kept moving.

Keep moving.

Keep moving.

Once I had pulled James, inch by painful inch, onto the bank, I checked to make sure he was still breathing. Putting my ear to his chest, I heard a slow but steady heartbeat and sighed heavily in relief. Calling his name, I couldn't seem to wake him. My shoulders shook in the cold air and I looked around for anything to make a fire. Not that I would know what to do once I found anything. There was something James did with a rock, but I had no idea what.

I stood quickly and stomped my feet to get some feeling to come back into my legs. There must be some wood around here. I'd deal with the fire part when it came to that.

Around the curve of the shoreline I found a pile of old driftwood that looked dry. I at least had enough sense to know that wet wood wouldn't burn. I gathered as much as I could carry before hearing a faint voice calling my name. I gripped the wood tighter and ran back to where I had left James.

He was sitting up and looking around, clearly disoriented. I dropped the wood and he turned at the sound, startled to see me. Standing quickly, he immediately put a hand to the side of his head and winced, closing his eyes in pain. My hands instinctively reached out to him as I approached before I snatched them back self-consciously.

"What happened?" he asked, opening one eye and trying to focus.

I looked up at him and shifted my weight once before answering.

"I guess you could say I saved you."

His eyes met mine in surprise and I laughed nervously.

"I know, I know, it seems impossible. But you'll just have to take my word for it. Well, that and the fact that you're alive." My voice caught a little on the last word as the enormity of what had happened seemed to hit me all at once.

James took one step toward me before stopping. I looked up at him while my breath hitched on a little suppressed cry. Eventually, he sat down again and I joined him.

I crinkled my nose and gave him a half-smile before I started to shiver. We were both still wet and the breeze was chilly.

James pulled me to him and tried to warm me by vigorously rubbing my arms and back.

We sat like that for a while, both trying to get warm while avoiding questions that hung heavily between us.

My mind had finally caught up with my rash actions. What had I done? I was betrothed to Damien. I didn't even know where he was. And here I was with James. I didn't even know where *we* were. I shut my eyes tightly against the queries I couldn't answer. I focused instead on the sound of James's heartbeat against my ear.

"Claire?"

I felt his heartbeat quicken slightly.

"Yes?"

"What *happened*?" he asked.

I slowly met his perplexed eyes. "I don't really know . . . The oar hit your head and you went over the side. I tried to get to you, but the water sucked you under so fast . . ." I didn't know how much to say about Damien's willingness to leave him to drown.

"Did you jump in after me? Where's Damien?"

I sighed. He was trying to make sense of something that was nonsensical. We both were. I didn't answer. I just looked up at him. And he looked down at me and swallowed.

His arms momentarily tightened, almost like a spasm of restless energy and then immediately relaxed. He loosed me abruptly and stood.

I could only see a sliver of his profile as he walked toward the river. He looked troubled and yet at the same time . . . some emotion I couldn't quite put my finger on. Resolved maybe?

He turned and walked back toward me. He crouched and took both of my hands in his, then waited until I dragged my eyes to meet his forceful gaze.

"Claire," he stuttered and started again. "I, Claire—I love you."

My heart lurched and I stopped breathing.

He continued, his eyes earnest, anxious. "I've fought it for as long as I could, but I think I started loving you that night at the ball when you demanded to know why I didn't like you." He smiled crookedly at the memory. "And it's not just because you're beautiful, or graceful, or whatever else your gifts say that you are. It's . . . more." His head raised and he looked me straight in the eyes. "You were brave enough to insist coming with us on this ridiculous quest and you're constantly putting needs of others before your own. Your nose wrinkles when you laugh at yourself. And when you smile, your eyes show it before your mouth does. I love the way you scowl when I count your freckles. And that you grew up swiping knives from servants." He shook his head and laughed nervously. "I even love the way you fall all over yourself and then blush because you're not used to being clumsy. I love being there to catch you, to protect you, but even more, I love that you've saved me. You've made me feel more like myself than I have in longer than I can remember. I don't know if this makes sense, but, Claire— It's just . . . *you*."

My eyes filled with tears. He saw them and squeezed my hands tighter. The hope I saw in his eyes made me burst into undignified sobs, and he had the nerve to smile.

He hesitantly leaned toward me, glancing at my eyes, trying to gauge my reaction. My heart pounded as he drew even nearer. He was about to kiss me. I knew he was.

And that's when it hit me. A kiss. *The* kiss. The one that was supposed to have ended the curse. And my family. I had to save them. And saving them was marrying Damien, not James.

"I'm sorry," I choked out, shaking my head just before his lips touched mine.

James pulled away, startled.

"I can't," I said again. "I'm sorry."

"You can't what?"

"I have to marry Damien. I belong with him. That's how it is meant to be."

James let go of my hands and backed away slowly. He looked worried, unbelieving. "You *really* think you could marry him?"

I shrugged helplessly.

Then he was there again, right in front of me, taking my face between his hands. His eyes were intense, pleading.

"Claire, you can't. You're too . . . He's—" His voice faltered.

My vision blurred as I tried to control my tears. I had to do this for my family.

"Well, this doesn't really concern you, does it? I *will* marry him, and you cannot stop me." I spoke harshly, biting back a sob.

He dropped his hands abruptly. He walked away and I saw his shoulders rise and fall as he tried to control his breathing. I exhaled, my shoulders sagging. I thought it was finished, but then he spun back and crossed the short distance between us. He grasped my arms and looked at me, hard.

He just looked. Neither of us said a word. I couldn't turn away. I was frozen in place.

Just then a voice rang out in the near distance.

It called my name.

Damien came crashing through the brush into our clearing.

"What's going on?" he demanded.

James let me go and walked to the river's edge. I saw again that same hardening in his eyes that I had noticed before in the way James often looked at Damien. Of course I had no answer to his question. At least none that Damien wanted to hear.

"I found James," I blurted out.

"So I see," he replied coolly. He walked over to James to grasp him by the shoulder. "Glad to see you're alright." I shivered at the coldness in his voice.

James didn't respond.

"How did you find us? Where's the boat?" I asked.

"The boat's fine. I secured it at the dock," Damien answered. "The water actually calmed down soon after you fell in."

Damien emphasized the word "fell" and I glanced at James just in time to see his jaw muscle clench.

Damien put his arm possessively around my waist and I gritted my teeth. Thoughts of my family forced my head onto his shoulder. I didn't look at James. I couldn't.

CHAPTER TWENTY-TWO

I sat, staring at the bright orange flames flickering and jumping, trying to sooth my aching head. Damien lounged on the other side of the fire, and I tried to block out the image of his hideously perfect face, concentrating harder on the part of the fire that turns blue, the part right next to the logs.

After finding us near the bridge, Damien had led us back to where he had tied up the boat. James and I couldn't look at each other. James's hatred and frustration was so thick it was nearly palpable. The beach near the lake was rocky and plagued by a cold breeze. However, Damien wouldn't hear of moving a bit further from the water to make camp, although I'm sure he saw the sense in it. He seemed desperate to be in control of the situation, so I acquiesced to his demands and James had no choice other than going along with us. James made a fire while Damien ranted on about how pointless this stupid quest had been from the beginning. We were nowhere nearer finding out how to stop the relapse now than we had been before setting off from the castle ten days ago. Had it really been that long? How much more time did we have? I felt my spirits drop lower and lower with every word Damien said. I caught James's eye

164

just once. He looked so concerned for my feelings and yet hurt and angry at the same time. I felt tears rush to my eyes and I had to look quickly away. James stalked off to the water's edge and I stared back at the fire.

Why had our search led us here? It didn't make sense, and something didn't feel right. *I* didn't feel right. My usually energetic body felt weak and listless. It wasn't just the normal exhaustion you might expect after a long and life-threatening journey. It was different, wrong. We were running out of time. By now everyone might have already relapsed. Who was next? Me?

In exasperation I pulled myself up and walked back toward the woods.

"Aurora," Damien demanded. I glanced at him over my shoulder and said, "I'll be back in a minute. I just need to be alone for a moment."

I stumbled along until I could no longer see the campfire and leaned against a tall pine tree. My breathing was quick and erratic. The damp, cool quiet of the forest did nothing to restore desperately needed peace and reassurance; I couldn't force my thoughts to settle.

Why had James said it? What was he thinking? What was I supposed to do now? It was easier to pretend like nothing was wrong when I thought he didn't have those feelings for me. How was I supposed to go on pretending now?

I couldn't keep convincing myself that I was happy with the life that was custom-made for me by someone else. But that was what had to happen, wasn't it? Everything else I had been promised at my birth had come true whether I wanted it to or not. I hadn't chosen to never miss a dance step or to paint a landscape or portrait with every brushstroke in place. I hadn't asked for a voice that wouldn't sing out of tune even if I tried. I had never had the choice. It always happened as they said, and I had always been fine with that, hadn't I? Now I hated that those things were disappearing, didn't I?

Long-repressed feelings of helplessness flooded my entire being and I started to shake. My fate was set. I had to marry Damien. I had to save my family, my kingdom. They were all falling back under the spell. A secret fear that *I* was to blame rose up and laughed garishly

165

at my turmoil. In my heart I had silently rebelled against my future with Damien for a long time.

"I'm sorry. I'm sorry," I mouthed, mutely.

My body continued to shake. I felt my strength weakening. I didn't know how or what to hold on to.

Suddenly, I heard the great rushing of wind and powerful roaring oceans that I had heard when I awakened from the spell. Only this time it was as though it was all being sucked into me instead of bursting out. I felt strangled and suffocated. My vision started to fade. Black spots darted in front of my eyes. I grasped the tree trunk, needing to hold on to something steady, needing to feel the rough, real bark beneath my hands. I squeezed until the soft skin of my palms started to split and crack, but I paid no attention.

I saw myself growing up at the castle. Confined. Protected. I had never questioned. I had always known my fate.

She shall be given the gift of grace.
She shall be given the gift of beauty.
She shall be given the gift of song.

This is what I am. What I have. Never what I choose.

She shall be given the gift of creativity.
She shall be given the gift of delicacy.
She shall be given the gift of sweetness.

I saw myself trembling as I wandered the castle hallway until hypnotically I touched the spindle and sank into oblivion.

She shall prick her finger on her sixteenth birthday and die.
She shall but sleep for a hundred years until a kiss awakens her to life and love.

The roaring grew louder, more insistent. I grabbed my head as I felt myself sinking. I fought to stay conscious.

No! That isn't who I am. That isn't all of me. James had seen *me*. The parts I had made myself.

I didn't want Damien. I wanted to be good at something on my own. I wanted to choose something on my own. I wanted . . .

Suddenly James was at my side, steadying me.

Of course. That's what he was here for.

I threw my head back and looked at him wildly, like a trapped animal searching for escape. His concerned, searching eyes told me I was strong and that I could do what I knew I must.

"I *choose* you. I want *you*. *I love you*," I gasped as I took his face between my trembling hands. Then, before the sleep claimed me once more, I brought his lips to mine.

The forest exploded around me. The roaring winds and oceans intensified even more, but now they burst out instead of caving in. My body felt light and free. My head cleared, and I saw pure love blinding me.

James's arms encircled me tightly as he returned my kiss with his own.

Real, electrifying life ran through me. I was rejuvenated. I *chose* James. With *him* was my life because *I chose* that it should be.

He pulled back just a little and I heard him whisper, "I love you too, Claire. You know I do." Then he gently brought my head to his shoulder, ran his hands along my tangled hair, and gave the sweetest, most contented sigh I had ever heard and my heart nearly leapt out of my chest to dance with his.

I could have stayed in James's arms forever, but some irritating noise was pulling me out of whatever heavenly daydream I was in. It was my name. The irritating part was the voice calling my name, and more importantly the person in possession of that voice. Damien. I flinched when I realized he was coming. James's realization came a moment after mine and he dropped his arms from around my waist, but not before Damien came out of the trees into our clearing. He stopped short and his face became an ugly mask of astonishment and rage.

"James," he started, his voice very cold. "This is starting to get a bit ridiculous. What is your explanation this time? More self-defense lessons? More invisible lightning storms?"

James took my hand and squared his shoulders. I suppose I should have been more worried, but all I could think about was how much I loved those broad shoulders and how perfect it felt to have James's hand around mine.

"She doesn't love you, Damien," James told him. "She loves me."

Damien's mouth and jaw worked as though he were trying to bite back his angry retort. He pinched the bridge of his nose between his eyes as though he were warding off a headache.

"We've been through this, James," Damien said slowly as though speaking to a simpleton. "She loves me. She has to be with *me*. She has no choice."

"That's not true," I objected, stepping forward with my newly discovered boldness. "I *can* choose. I think that was the problem the whole time, the reason people were falling back into the sleep, I wasn't marrying my true love. James is my true love." I blushed. I think James and I were both blushing and looking very silly and happy while Damien fumed in front of us. I continued, trying to convince him.

"I was falling back too. I felt it coming, that same terrible falling, sinking feeling, but I fought it and I chose James. And then . . . I was free. I have a feeling everyone back home is free as well. It's as though a huge weight has been lifted from me."

Damien rolled his eyes patronizingly.

"How poetic, darling." He looked back and forth at me and James. Then he stepped closer to James.

"So, now you'll be a prince, I suppose? It's rare that a . . . *knight* makes that leap in rank." I felt James's body tense and I looked up at him.

"That doesn't matter to me, and it certainly won't matter to my father. Especially after the curse has been lifted for good," I stated firmly.

Damien ignored my comment. He kept his eyes on James and continued, "I'm sure your poor family will miss you dreadfully. And that charming sister of yours . . . What was her name? Elise? Ah yes . . . She'll be very lonely." Damien's face was twisted in an ugly smirk. I felt James's body go rigid now. He was almost shaking with the effort of suppressed movement. I didn't quite understand what was going on.

"James," I assured him, "Your family can come live with us in the palace." My words didn't comfort him. He acted as though he hadn't even heard me. The two men glared at each other. James felt so tense beside me I thought he might explode with the strain. I took a breath to again try to smooth things over between the two when I suddenly jumped, startled out of my mind. James's arms instinctually went around me in protection as usual, only this time he kept them there instead of dropping them quickly back to his sides as he had always done before.

A huddled figure with frizzy red hair had appeared out of nowhere.

"You've figured it out, dearie!" Bernadette screeched as she launched herself at me and James in a fiery embrace.

James and Damien looked as shocked by her presence as I was.

"You've discovered the true meaning on my gift!" she enthused. "The kiss awakens you to life and love. Life! I wanted you to discover life as it should be. Unpredictable. Exciting. Full of love and uncertainty and choices. Damien's kiss awoke you, but it was James who helped you discover life and true love." She looked as though she might burst with pride. "I can't wait to tell those prudish little snits at the council that my gift worked. It truly was the best of all," she crowed gleefully.

I could barely gather my thoughts enough to speak. "So it's really over?" I croaked.

"Of course it is, my sweet!" she pulled my face down to her level and placed a loud, smacking kiss on my cheek. She released me and my foot slipped as I straightened. James, as always, steadied me before I fell. Still clumsy? I groaned and turned to him for inspection.

"How many freckles?" I demanded.

He grinned and kissed my nose.

I turned to Bernadette.

"So, I'm guessing I don't get my old gifts back," I grumbled.

"Of course not!" she smiled triumphantly. "I would never subject you to living with those monstrosities. Nothing but a bunch of useless excuses for fairy gifts."

I considered pouting, but thought better of it. Now was hardly the time to focus on loss when I had gained so much. I let James kiss my nose again and then leaned down for another hug from Bernadette.

"Thank you for everything," I whispered in her ear. "Please feel welcome at our kingdom for anything you could ever want."

"Thank you, sweet, but I'm quite content on my mountain. Aside from you and your James, I'm still thoroughly disenchanted with the human race." She turned to Damien. I confess I'd completely forgotten about him brooding off to the side. "As for you, sir," she scowled up at him. "I'll thank you to leave these two alone and mind your own business."

It was clear Bernadette was not fond of Damien.

He opened and closed his mouth in frustration. He seemed unsure of what to say or how to even react to this. He spun on his heel and stomped back to camp. I turned to Bernadette and gave her one last hug.

"See you at the wedding. Oh, there are shortcuts to get home, dearie." She explained them quickly, touched my cheek in farewell, and then scurried behind a group of trees, disappearing to who knows where.

I lingered a bit and held James back as well.

"Damien is furious," I said softly.

James only nodded tightly and started back to camp.

"Wait," I called softly. James turned to look back at me, but he seemed distracted. I felt foolish. What was I expecting? After such an emotional revelation this hardly seemed any way to end the day. "Never mind," I mumbled, feeling silly and I followed him through the trees. A few paces from the campfire, James darted behind a tree with me in tow. He gave me an abbreviated version of our former kiss, looked into my eyes, smiled crookedly, and squeezed my shoulders before releasing me and continuing toward the fire. I couldn't meet Damien's eye as I walked slowly into my tent.

CHAPTER TWENTY-THREE

*T*he following morning dawned bright and shimmery. Was it just my imagination or did the sun cast a glow that caused everything around me to glitter? Stranger things had happened in this wild forest. Today we would be home. I would see my father and mother awake and whole. James stood and smiled at me when I emerged from my tent and my heart gave a great roll inside my chest. I walked right up to him and smiled at him until he pulled me to him and tucked my head under his chin. My heart sighed before my lungs did.

"Nice braid," I heard his teasing voice rumble inside his chest as he tugged my hair.

"Good morning to you too," I answered, my own voice muffled by said chest.

He leaned down, pressed a light kiss on my nose, and released me. I turned toward the stream just as I heard him say, "Two more." I shifted back and pretended to glare at him.

"You wouldn't happen to be talking about my freckles, would you? Keeping count again?" I narrowed my eyes even as I barely contained a huge smile.

"That's what I'm here for," he laughed and nudged me toward the stream.

I splashed my face with cold water just as I heard someone clearing their throat behind me and I jumped up. It was Damien. He stood looking at me with a strange look in his eyes. I sighed uneasily and stepped toward him.

"Damien," I began, "I truly am sorry about how things ended between us. I wanted to speak to you before privately and explain, but then everything happened so fast."

"So explain," Damien prodded. "We're meant to be together, Aurora."

"That's just it," I tried again. "I've asked you to call me Claire. Everyone else I am close to calls me Claire because I prefer it. You always call me Aurora simply because you think it's prettier. And I let you because I thought I had to. But I want to be Claire. I'm not Aurora. I'm just not."

"But—" Damien started before I interrupted him.

"Didn't you hear what Bernadette said?"

"This is between you and me," he insisted.

"That's true, but she said everything I had been feeling yet didn't know how to express. I have had to go along with someone else's idea of happily every after my whole life and I finally realized that wasn't living at all. Perfect and happy don't always add up to be the same thing. I finally broke Zora's curse once and for all when I decided to take my life into my own hands and choose how I wanted my life to be."

Damien's brow furrowed, though in anger or sorrow I couldn't tell.

"Why not talk to me? You never gave me any indication there was something wrong," he argued.

"I was in denial myself, but you had to see we weren't happy with each other. We never laugh or talk. Maybe we did a little back at the castle, but at the first sign of trouble any friendship or relationship crumbled. So long as I was quiet and docile and still had all my gifts, yes, we were fine. But that's— that's just not the real me."

Damien looked distracted. He seemed lost in his own thoughts as I tried to communicate mine. I shrugged helplessly and reached out to touch his arm. His eyes turned hard and shot up to look at mine.

"Now you listen to me," Damien hissed through clenched teeth. "You will not marry James. It's out of the question. We will proceed with our wedding as planned."

I tried to shake my arm free and I felt his fingers dig in harder, bruising my skin.

"Damien, you're hurting me," I said firmly. "Haven't you been paying attention to anything that's happened? I can't and *won't* marry you. Not in a thousand years. I chose James because I love him. That's how we broke the spell."

"I'm sorry," Damien let me go and started laughing, only there was no mirth in the sound. "This isn't supposed to happen. This can't be happening. There is just no way that a farmer is getting what I want."

"What are you even talking about?" I demanded.

"Listen, I don't think you realize the state of my kingdom. We are on the brink of revolution. My idiot of a father cannot control such a large kingdom. Our treasury is nearly empty and we need this alliance to go through."

"I'm sure we can work something out. Perhaps the borders can go back to the way they were and we could help your kingdom somehow."

"It's been a hundred years, Aurora. Generations have passed. You can't simply erase that and have everything go back the way it was." His tone was both condescending and frantic. His eyes were starting to take on a wild look.

James entered our clearing at that moment and came directly to my side. I looked up at him gratefully. Damien turned on James with fury.

"And you," he accused, shoving his finger in James's face. "How could you? How could you steal her from me? I thought we were friends."

"When have we ever been friends, Your Highness?" James asked pointedly.

"How can you ask that after all I've given you?" Damien scoffed.

"Very easily," James growled.

"Hold on," I interrupted. "What is going on?"

"Aurora—Claire," Damien glanced at me. "Perhaps James can enlighten you on how he came to become a knight."

James tensed beside me.

"Fine," I exclaimed. "Let him tell me. I don't know how I can explain it to you any clearer. Nothing you can do will stop me. I choose James, Damien. I love him."

Damien's eyes were taking on a wild look. Like an animal backed into a corner. James took my hand. Damien's eyes darted down to our joined hands, then back to my face.

"That's where you're wrong, Aurora. I think I can stop you. Because of your love for James." He turned his gaze to James. "You know I hold your family in high esteem, dear fellow. Let's not do anything to jeopardize that." He turned on his heel and stalked away.

I felt the air slowly go out of James next to me and I whirled to face him.

"Enough secrets. Enough strange, veiled threats between you two. What is going on?" He started to turn away and I placed a hand on his cheek to force him to look at me.

"No," I shook my head. "It's time I know everything."

James sighed and slowly nodded. He led me to a stone where I sat down. Apparently this was going to be a long explanation. He looked off in the distance and I waited.

After a deep breath, James began. "I was born James of Baudouin, on a small but prosperous farm near one of the border towns of what was once your kingdom. It was a time of political unrest. King Cyrille, Damien's father, is a carousing buffoon who doesn't know the first thing about governing a kingdom, especially a kingdom as large as his. I grew up hearing my father speak disparagingly of tyranny and all the evil and unfairness that the monarchy represented. Our farm gradually became less and less successful as tax collectors and ruffians stole from our profits. When I was eighteen years old, my father left to travel to Gaël to protest our treatment and he put me in charge of the farm and the family. My mother, Breona, and my sister, Eleanor, and I bade him farewell and wished him good luck on his journey." James paused here to swallow.

"He never returned. A neighboring farmer came home missing a leg and an eye and told us that my father had been killed by royal guards in a riot. The sorrow and anger in my heart grew and grew until it nearly took over my very existence. I felt I had to travel to the city to avenge his death and finish what he started. My mother and sister begged me not to go, but I ignored their tearful pleadings and left to satisfy the vengeful needs of my anger and hate."

When he paused again I squeezed his hand once, urging him to continue.

"Once I reached the city I was overwhelmed by the bustle and activity. I had never left my small village and had never seen anything like it. I was young and naïve and I didn't even know how to begin to fight my father's battle. While dining in an inn, a few nights after my arrival I heard a scuffle in a nearby room. I went to investigate and saw a very angry innkeeper attacking a well-dressed young man who appeared defenseless. The innkeeper was armed and, of course, my sense of injustice flared. I was strong as my father had been before me. A life of heavy manual labor had only made me more so. I knocked out the innkeeper and rushed the well-dressed man out a back door, into a quiet alleyway.

"The man thanked me and invited me to dine with him at his home to show his gratitude. I counted myself fortunate and accepted gladly.

"It was only after we reached the palace gates that I realized that this man might be more than simply a well-dressed merchant or shop owner. I heard the guards address him as "Your Highness" and I asked him who he was. He introduced himself as Prince Damien and I froze. I had never heard my father speak ill of the prince, but he was royalty and my father had lumped them all together in a group of villains and cheats. Prince Damien, however, seemed kind. I was dazzled by the sumptuous food and surroundings and the music and people. For a while I nearly forgot my once felt duty to my father and the family I had left behind."

James looked at me, almost as if to see if I was disappointed in him. I nodded reassuringly.

"Go on," I urged.

James cleared his throat and continued.

"Damien provided me with room and board and enlisted my services in training with him. He paid me handsomely and I sent everything I earned home to my mother and sister, thinking that made it alright that I had, in a way, abandoned them. I became trained in the arts of courtly fighting. I learned to wield a sword and handle a dagger with as much ease as farming tools. I quickly saw that my skill far surpassed the prince's. He was uninterested in perfecting any of these abilities. He did not like to do anything he had to work at. And what I came to see he was good at was charming people. More particularly, women. By the time I had been away from home for nearly a year I began to see him for what he really was. At first I tried to rationalize his behavior, but I could feel my disgust for him and his way of life constantly growing. Whenever I would broach the subject, Damien steered our conversation away and offered me something like a larger room or a more generous living. He eventually knighted me and appointed me his personal companion and protector. I continued to send money from my earnings home to my mother and sister and tried to convince myself that I was helping them by staying at the palace.

"On one occasion after I'd been at the castle for a little over a year and a half, I went to dine with some friends at the inn where I had first met the prince. The innkeeper had changed and when I inquired over what happened to the previous owner, I found out that he had been executed for attacking a member of the royal family. Treason. But then I heard that the less official reason was that the prince had forced his attentions on the innkeeper's wife and had been caught by the woman's husband, who, in his indignation, attacked him. Now, the innkeeper's widow lives in squalid conditions, destitute and ruined."

"That wasn't your fault, you know," I interrupted. I could tell by the tightness of his face he still blamed himself for reading that initial situation incorrectly.

"I shouldn't have gotten involved. I should have seen through Damien so much earlier. Much earlier. How could I have been so duped?" His eyes turned to me, full of shame and regret.

"Very easily," I tried to reassure him. "You were young and hurting from the loss of your father. You had so many feelings of anger and frustration and no clear direction for them. Of course you were susceptible to his manipulations."

James appeared unconvinced. I tried again.

"Besides, you could ask the same of me. How could I have fallen for his act? I was promised a happily ever after and I was ready to blindly believe anything. But life is rarely as clear-cut as that. People are complicated. It's not that easy."

His slow nod encouraged me. "What did you do next?" I asked.

He took a breath and began again.

"I confronted Damien that very night. Our words grew heated and I threatened to leave and join the growing armies of unhappy subjects threatening revolution. That was when he started making veiled threats to my family. I was caught in his trap and I knew there was no way to escape without endangering them.

"When he heard of a barricaded castle with a sleeping princess and an unrivaled treasure he insisted that we search for it. He's very superstitious and he became obsessed with the legend. He was convinced that if he didn't find it, someone else would and he knew how much his kingdom needed money. I resisted, but he again threatened my family, this time bringing them to the castle as prisoners and I was not permitted to see them. He promised that if I accompanied him as his guard and did nothing to derail his plan he would release me from our agreement and my family and I would be free to live in peace. The majority of his father's armies were needed to subdue riots and protect the castle from revolutionaries so he traveled with me as his only companion and source of protection. We took additional measures and disguised ourselves as a nobleman and his valet.

"When we finally reached the tremendous thorn wall, he instructed me to begin cutting a path through it. I expected hard work since Damien had warned me that many had tried to get through the impressive thorns, but none had succeeded. At the first touch of my sword, the thorns and branches fell easily to the side. Each subsequent strike from the blade created an easy walkway for Damien and me to go through. As soon as we reached the inside, we turned in astonishment to find that the great wall was slowly dwindling and shrinking until nothing remained.

"The castle itself was in a state of ruin and disrepair. Moss and ivy covered nearly every inch of the stone walls and towers. We crossed a rickety drawbridge over an empty moat and entered the musty courtyard. Bodies littered the ground. I examined several bodies more closely and found that they were warm, breathing, perfectly preserved, although extremely dirty and covered with dust and grime. They really were all sleeping. No amount of shaking or yelling could rouse a single one of them. Damien insisted that we move on to find the sleeping princess. We climbed endless towers and searched enumerable hallways, but we found no one to fit the description that Damien had read of."

I listened in fascination. I had never really heard this side of my story before.

"As dusk approached," James continued, "I tried to reason with a furious Damien that he must have been mistaken. He refused to give up. I leaned against a rotting, wooden door as I watched him rage and felt a slight give. I turned to examine the door more closely. It was covered with dust and the lock looked flimsy. I stepped back and then kicked the door in. It collapsed easily and we climbed the stairs to a room higher than any of the others. Within that was only a large bed in the center of the room covered with layers of gauzy canopy. We saw the form of a sleeping girl and Damien excitedly pulled the flimsy sheets away until we got our first glimpse of you. The canopy had kept you clean for the most part. Of course I noticed your beauty, but I hadn't expected anything else. Once Damien kissed you we waited until your eyelids began fluttering and you began making those horrible scratchy, witchlike noises."

We both smiled at the memory.

"We thought you might not be able to speak until we realized you were asking for water. You started talking about how nice it was to meet us and good it was of us to come and all this happily ever after kind of nonsense like you had expected us. I thought you must be insane, but Damien played along and before long the two of you were engaged and the castle was on its way to renovation.

"I assumed you were no different from any other royal I had met and dismissed you without another thought. There were a few times when you let that facade slip and I saw a glimpse of someone worth knowing and it frightened me so I tried to stay away. That was why I was so cold to you. I didn't want to like you or respect you or even enjoy your company. I wanted to keep my negative image and perception of royalty intact. It made things so much simpler. But you slowly got under my skin and made me like you in spite of myself. What finally changed my opinion of you the most was your determination and bravery in the face of the spell's return. I had never associated royalty with any kind of bravery or honor."

I interrupted once more to give James a quick kiss on his cheek.

He smiled at me before continuing. "Once we became friends I tried to convince myself that was enough, but Damien would speak of you in ways that made me want to strangle him. I knew that I wouldn't be able to stand it if I stood by and watched you marry him. One day, after Damien found us hiding from the lightning storm in the cave, he tricked me into walking in on him kissing you after he'd told me that I was making a fool of myself by being so attentive to you. He said that if you knew what I really was, you would want nothing to do with me. I tried to distance myself then. But that was when Damien saved you from the flying trunks and I hated myself for nearly letting you get killed. Seeing you in Damien's arms when he rescued you, when he had never rescued anything in his life, nearly made me lose my mind. But then you saved me in the Glass Lake and I felt there might some hope for me after all."

When James had finished speaking I wiped a tear from my eye. My heart ached for everything he had been through.

"You can't think that I would care anything about where or how you grew up, can you?" I asked.

James remained somewhat hesitant but then shrugged and said, "It's a relief that you finally know—that I'm no longer hiding anything from you. However, I'm not so sure your father will see it your way."

"You're wrong," I insisted. "Their gratitude for what you've done for the kingdom and for me will make any details about your background completely inconsequential. And Damien did knight you, after all. He at least did that."

I looked at him and furrowed my brow. "You two always did seem a strange pair," I mused. "I could see you were opposites in almost every way. And yet, I actually do believe he considered you friends." When James's head reared up in protest, I quickly added, "In his way."

"How can you even think that?" James asked.

"Think about it," I started. "The life of a royal can be very alienating. Although surrounded by constant attention, you have very little opportunity to actually connect with people. And if his parents were as bad as you say, he probably had little to no teaching toward any way other than selfishness. Did you ever see him with a friend?"

James gave a bark of bitter laughter. "Everyone was his friend. Everyone did just as he said."

I looked at him until he conceded.

"No, he didn't. Not a real friend."

"So, maybe that explains a few things."

James started shaking his head again and I put up my hand.

"I'm not justifying anything he has done, you know me better than that. I'm just saying that if we know his motivations, his shortcomings, his upbringing, we can better understand how he thinks and how we can stop him."

James nodded.

"His is one head I really don't want to look into," he all but groaned.

"I know," I sympathized. "So, what do we do now? We seem to be back under Damien's thumb. If he has your family . . . and I really cannot marry him—"

"No," James interrupted swiftly. "You can't."

"But maybe we play along? To some degree. Until we figure out a way to stop him?"

James slowly nodded.

"Don't worry," he tried to reassure me. "I—we will find a way."

I smiled at his change in pronoun.

"And what on earth can you find to smile about right now?" James asked, fighting a smile in spite of himself.

"You. And me when I'm with you. And that you call me Claire. And that we're going to do this together." I snuggled my head on his shoulder, finding a strange sense of contentment amidst the danger.

Unfortunately, Damien's footsteps to the side of us brought me back to reality with a jolt. James and I stood to face him.

"I've decided something," Damien began, as though addressing his servants. "We will not go back to Kalynbrae. We will go to Gaël. I'm sure once you see how things are there, you will realize that you must follow through on our original agreement."

James started to protest, knowing how important it was to me to see my family, but I stopped him.

"Alright, we'll go."

With the shortcut I had learned from Bernadette the journey to Gaël would be under a day's travel. Somehow Bernadette had arranged for our horses to be just at the other side of the forest where one direction would take us to my home and the other, to Damien's.

The journey seemed interminable due to the tense silence between the three of us. James took little opportunities to throw me a look or smile here and there to let me know we were okay. Damien kept his eyes on the road.

CHAPTER TWENTY-FOUR

We reached Gaël just before nightfall. We rode up to a quiet, relatively unused gate in the city wall. Unlike at Kalynbrae, where the castle sat in a much more rural setting outside of town, Gaël's palace was at the heart of a large city. James told us to stay back in the trees as he went to feel out the situation with the gatekeeper.

"Why don't we simply ride in?" I asked Damien in confusion.

"Things aren't as idyllic here as what you're used to," Damien smiled wryly.

James came back and quickly retrieved our cloaks from our packs.

"Put these on," he commanded, tying on his own and making sure the hood shadowed half his face. I almost smiled as I recognized the calm, take-charge James from the beginning of our journey.

"Yes, sir," I saluted teasingly, and secured my cloak. He glanced at me in surprise before grinning and pulling my hood forward.

"The situation has only escalated since our departure. It's in our best interest to attempt to fit in," he explained. "Like that night in the inn. Try to forget you're a princess for a while."

Damien looked up in annoyed interest at not knowing what we were talking about. I shrugged and turned away.

Once we all had our faces partially hidden, we quietly walked toward the gate, leading our horses behind us. James took the lead and spoke again with the gatekeeper. He gestured toward us and the gatekeeper waved us forward. I held my breath as we walked through, although I didn't even know what I was afraid of. This was Damien's kingdom. Why were we hiding? Once out of earshot from the gatekeeper, James spoke in low tones to us.

"Every gate is different as far as loyalties go. There was no way to guess which way that man leaned politically until speaking with him, and once I found out he was a rebel supporter there wasn't anyway I could back out without him getting suspicious. I told him you were rebel sympathizing nobles who had valuable information to the cause."

"And he bought that?" Damien asked.

"The people are desperate, Your Highness. They'll believe what they want to hear."

By this time we were well and truly inside the city. I had kept my head down until now, focusing on the movement of James's boots in front of me. I now noticed sounds and smells quite foreign to me. The smell of unclean bodies, sweat, smoke, and sickness filled the air. I could hear the sound of men yelling, babies crying, raucous laughter, and an occasional screech piercing the air. I dared a glance around me and saw the greatest poverty I had ever seen. The cobblestone streets were filthy, the buildings in horrible disrepair, the people ragged. I swallowed and kept my head down.

We walked toward the castle as James neatly sidestepped and guided us through the mayhem that was Damien's capitol city.

"I had no idea it would be like this," I breathed.

James glanced behind him with a look of understanding and Damien made some sort of noise behind me. We kept walking.

Suddenly a man came flying straight for me out of the door of the tavern on our right. I gasped as the heavy force knocked me to the ground. In a jumble of arms and legs, James and Damien struggled to free me from the inebriated man who had landed on me. Once he realized he was tangled with a woman, his foggy gaze turned lecherous.

"Well, what do we have here?" he slurred, his breath foul.

My stomach roiled as I shoved him away from me. I thought to use one of James's tactics and quickly snapped my stiff hand into the underside of his nose. He howled and lunged for me, just before James got a grip on his arm and yanked him away from me.

"Back away," James warned, holding the man by his lapels and then shoving him from himself with such force he fell backward onto his back and nearly up over his head. He sat up as James was helping me dust myself off and making sure I was uninjured.

"Here, aren't you that fellow that hangs around with the prince?" The man said in a groan as he held his head.

James and Damien froze.

"You have me confused with someone else," James said gruffly. "I wouldn't be caught dead with that swine."

The man got up to get a closer look, but James turned away under the guise of calming the horses. The man then turned to examine Damien and in a flash I realized that in the scuffle, Damien's hood had been knocked off. The man's eyes widened.

"It's—Why, It's the prince," he started yelling. James quickly delivered a punch to the man's jaw that knocked him out cold, but not before an onlooker from inside the tavern could take notice. He took up the yelling and a crowd started for the door.

"Run," James looked at me. The noise from the tavern escalated as people started pouring out. "Damien, take the horses and Claire and run for The Black Lantern," James yelled. I tried to protest, but Damien grabbed my hand and the reins and ran. I tried to look back as we made our mad escape. I could see James delivering devastating blows to the crowd one after another as they tried to rush around him. There had to be more than ten men. Tears stung my eyes as I realized he was sacrificing his own safety for the sake of our getaway. I yanked on my hand, trying to free myself.

"Aurora, he'll be alright. James has gotten himself out of much worse scrapes than this," Damien said through clenched teeth as he tried to urge me to continue.

"Because of you," I screeched back at him.

"If you don't hurry, they'll get to us and it will only make it harder on James. He can't defend us if we don't get away."

Finally reason reached me and I followed, tears streaming down my face.

Out of breath and several blocks away, we finally slowed our pace.

"These horses are drawing attention to us," Damien growled. "There's a stable coming up on the left. You need to go in and arrange for them to house the horses until further notice. Just say, um, three day's time." He shoved the reins into my hands and pointed at the building while he hid in the alleyway. I tried to calm my breathing as I approached the livery and spoke to the man in the front. He didn't pay much attention to me. I must have been dirtier than I thought. I paid the man in advance, gave Angeline's name, and quickly hurried back to Damien.

"Good," Damien said when he saw me empty handed. "Come on, let's go." He led me into another dirty alleyway and I cringed at the smells we encountered.

"I have a question," I huffed. "James yelled our meeting place back there, so what is to stop anyone from following us?"

"That's not the real name. The Black Lantern is code for a small inn called Weary Traveler. It's near the castle. I know my way around there. It's where James and I met. At one point I wanted to throw him off of some search for the inn and I told him the wrong name, hoping to foil his plans. He knew I'd remember."

I swallowed my disgust as I thought of why Damien knew his way around and why James had felt honor-bound to search for the inn when he found out more and more of Damien's true character.

We reached a decrepit building and Damien pushed me though a side door into a dark hallway where we waited. We waited for what seemed like hours. I heard the door creak and I stiffened. Damien grabbed my arm to still any sudden movements, but he needn't have bothered. I felt paralyzed. I saw a large form enter the hallway and I held my breath. Then the form turned and whispered my name.

Something like a strangled sob left my throat and I threw myself at James, clinging to him in relief. His arms quickly came around me.

"You made it," he breathed.

"How did *you* make it?" I demanded incredulously. "There were probably a dozen men against one."

"I told you he's been in worse scrapes before, Aurora." Damien insisted.

"Let's just say it's a good thing I'm familiar with the rooftops in this city," James explained. I hugged him tighter.

"Where are the horses?" James asked.

"They were drawing attention to us, so Damien had me leave them at a livery on the way here," I answered.

"Good thinking," James rubbed his chin and motioned for us to go into a back storage room. He found a candle and lit it, illuminating a small, cool room with shelves of ale kegs lining the walls.

"Why couldn't we have met at the castle if it's so close to here?" I asked.

"Aurora, James couldn't very well have yelled out, 'Meet at the castle,' could he?" Damien's tone was condescending and I flushed. "Not to mention the castle gates are teeming with protestors and rebels."

"She prefers Claire," James said through his teeth. "Call her Claire."

"Well, *I* prefer Aurora," Damien bit out.

"Well, no one cares what *you* prefer," James retorted.

"How dare—"

"Alright, let's move on from that," I scolded both of them. "So, what now?"

"We wait," James answered. "Just until we make sure no one is on our trail. Then we find a weak point and get into the castle."

"How long?" I yawned.

"I'll give it an hour. Feel free to get some rest. I will keep watch," James scooted over on his bench and made room for me next to him. I quickly settled down and put my head on his shoulder. I chanced a look over at Damien and through the dim light I could see his eyes glaring at us bitterly. I swallowed and shut my eyes once more.

CHAPTER TWENTY-FIVE

I woke with a start when James slowly stroked my cheek.

"Time to go," he whispered. "It's been all clear for nearly two hours."

I stretched my arms.

"I thought you wanted to leave after an hour," I covered another yawn.

"You looked so peaceful," he answered quietly.

"And you look sheepish," I teased. "Thank you." I glanced at Damien to find him still dozing and tilted my chin up for a quick kiss, which James seemed more than happy to provide.

We rose and James shook Damien.

"It's time to move."

Damien nodded and stood. James peeked out the door and then beckoned us to follow him.

We entered the alleyway soundlessly and I followed James as he maneuvered through the back passages between buildings, Damien picking up the rear. In minutes we reached where the buildings stopped and opened up to the square before the palace. I took in the scene before me. It must have been near midnight by now and the crowds were dissipating. We were nowhere near the main entrance, thankfully. Although of course that would have been intentional in James's plan. I saw James gesture to an area near a gate that had very little commotion and attention. Damien and I nodded. We walked casually toward the gate, trying to fit in with the few people still out. When we got near, Damien threw back his hood. The guards recognized him immediately and fumbled to open the gate as quickly as possible. Unfortunately, the meager crowd also recognized him and began to charge, but James was ready for them. He threw me behind him and backed us toward the gate just as the guards opened it and grabbed Damien and then me. James had to throw two punches before ducking in himself and grabbing me to follow Damien and leave the guards to the crowds now swarming the gate.

We rushed toward the door and entered into a magnificent hallway. I gasped at the opulence around me. Gold plaited pillars, lush draperies, sparkling mirrors, and rich paintings covered every surface. And this was only a back hallway. No wonder the kingdom was in ruin. Had they even considered downsizing to help the economy?

"Nice, isn't it?" Damien winked, all his swagger returning now that he was on familiar shores.

We made out way toward the main living quarters. Before we reached them we came to a room with guards posted at the door. Although it seemed not nearly grand enough to be the king's chambers, I assumed it must be. Damien greeted the guards and opened the door and James and I followed him inside. There were a few candles lit within, but it was still dark. I heard a feminine gasp and turned to see two women to my right rising from their chairs near a fireplace. They rushed toward James who opened his arms just as they threw themselves at him. I glanced back at Damien, who winked again and said, "We'll be in touch," before closing the door behind him. I heard a lock turn and a few muffled words to the guards on the other side of the door. I gasped and ran toward the door, pounding my fists and trying, in vain, to open the door.

James quickly joined me and kicked the door in frustration.

"What is it, James?" a pretty girl came up to him and held onto his hand. I scrunched my nose and tried to squash the sudden feeling of jealousy that rose in me.

"I'm not sure, El," he soothed, putting an arm around her.

El. Eleanor. This was his sister. Of course. I nearly smacked my forehead. I saw the freckles and smiled. The older woman joined us and I turned to face James's mother. She looked at me too. Then Eleanor followed suit. Of course, they had no idea who I was.

"Mother, El," James began, extending a hand to me, which I took gratefully, "This is Princess Aurora Claire of Kalynbrae. The sleeping princess."

I smiled at them as understanding dawned in their eyes.

"So you actually found her?" Eleanor clarified.

"We actually found her," James grinned. He then filled them in on everything that had been going on for the last month or so and they in turn let him know how things were going here.

"We don't hear much," his mother, Breonna, told us. "The guards keep a strict watch on us. We can rarely leave our quarters and when we do get a breath of fresh air, we are heavily guarded. But we've heard a few things from the servants. They say revolution is close. Things have gotten worse. The few royal supporters that were left have either fallen or joined the fight." She turned to add additional information for my benefit. "The problem is they don't have a clear leader. They don't have a plan. The people are simply angry and fed up with the injustices forced on them for the last decades. Rumor is now that they want the Duke of Ellsworth to come and take over the crown."

"Who is the Duke of Ellsworth?" I asked

"He's a cousin of Damien's. He's a good, level-headed man from what I hear. Damien can't stand him and that's enough of a recommendation for me," James smirked.

"Is he interested? Willing?" I pressed.

"It's difficult to get word to him," he explained.

"We heard just last week from a scullery maid that a rider may have gotten out to get to his estate. If he can reach him and gain an audience, there just might be a chance," Eleanor said with excitement.

James's mother yawned and he immediately helped her to her bed.

"You two should try and get some rest too," he smiled at me and Eleanor.

"You can share with me," she offered. "This bed is enormous. Much bigger than anything we had at home." I blushed to see it wasn't much larger than my own bed, one that I had never found overly large.

"Thank you so much," I took her hand in mine and squeezed it.

James dragged an armchair from the fireplace toward the door. He placed it directly in front and settled himself down, trying to get comfortable, while still remaining aware if someone were to come in. I really loved that man. As if reading my thoughts, he looked up at me, caught me staring, and sent me a smile that set those butterflies that had recently taken up residence in my stomach to dancing.

"Go ahead and sleep. I'll be fine."

"Thank you for protecting us. As usual," I smiled.

"That's what I'm here for," he quipped back and I threw him a pillow.

Eleanor rolled her eyes at us and laughed.

"I can't believe you fell for a princess, James."

"Believe it, El," he grinned and shut his eyes, ignoring both of us.

"Here, let me help you with your hair. Your, um, braid is in a sorry state," Eleanor led me to the vanity near her bed. I chuckled.

"It probably didn't look much better before all the action. I only recently learned to braid my own hair. In fact, your brother taught me."

Eleanor crowed in delight at that. "What else did my manly brother teach you?" she laughed.

"You two realize I can hear you, right? I'm right here," James grumbled from his seat.

I laughed and thanked Eleanor for fixing my braid. I fell into bed soon after and slept the moment my head hit the pillow.

I was fourteen years old and I was hiding in a cupboard. I knew I was much too old for this, but I couldn't stomach my art lesson today. It was merely a formality. Something to keep me busy. I already knew everything instinctively and both my tutor and I knew it. It was so uncomfortable. And I was so tired. I had stayed up all night reading. I stiffened as Angeline walked by my cupboard, calling my name. She passed and my eyes began to feel drowsy. They must have closed at some point. But then I saw them. Two glowing orbs that narrowed into slits. They were green. A strange green. They came closer, almost snapping at me. I screamed and fell out of the cupboard just as Angeline was making another round. She gathered me up, dusted me off and helped me to my art lesson. I refused to let my instructor use any green paint.

I woke from my dream with a soft gasp. It left me feeling unsettled. I blinked and rubbed my eyes. I could see the dawn through the small windows. The room filled with a soft light. I got up and poured myself some water. I noticed everyone was still asleep. I was actually surprised my quiet movements hadn't woken James. He was normally so attuned to any threat of danger. I wondered if he'd even had a real night's rest in, well, years. I walked over to him with a smile. His arms hung limply at his side and his mouth was just slightly open as deep breaths made his chest rise and fall. I couldn't resist pressing a quick kiss to his forehead.

"Wretched princess," he mumbled groggily. "Can't you see I'm trying to sleep?"

"Sorry," I grinned.

"I forgive you," he said, his eyes still closed.

"Thank you," I said gravely.

Finally a little smile turned half of his mouth up. "Good morning," he said, finally opening his eyes.

"Good morning," I smiled back, as I walked back to the washstand and bathed my face.

Eleanor began to stir as well as Breonna. We all freshened up and Eleanor let me borrow one of her dresses as mine had clearly seen better days. She was slightly taller than I, but it fit well and I thanked her for it.

"The maids will be in soon with breakfast," Breonna informed us. "You see, James, other than feeling liked trapped mice most of the time they treat us decently." Her tone was reassuring as though she was trying to alleviate any guilt he might be carrying for their situation. How well she knew her son.

The breakfast came in and we ate a simple meal together in relative silence. I placed a bench under the window after I had finished and tried to get a better view from the high window. Even from here, the city looked awful. You could practically sense the unrest in the air. I sighed heavily. The alliance would have presented a solution, I saw that now.

James came and stood next to me.

"What are you thinking about?" he asked.

"Am I being selfish?" I blurted. "Denying Damien this answer to all this kingdom's problems?" I stepped down from the bench and sat down dejectedly. James hesitated for a moment and then joined me.

"It's not that simple, Claire. Even if you two had married. Even if you became a strong and capable queen, which I'm sure you would and will. Damien is Damien. He will never be a fair or just ruler. With a king like that . . ." he trailed off.

I nodded in agreement, but the guilt still gnawed at me. James interpreted my silence as something else entirely.

"Look, if you're having second thoughts, if you're realizing you don't actually want to be tied to a farmer for the rest of your life—"

"James," I started to protest angrily, but he held a hand to stop me before continuing.

"There's nothing forcing you to marry me. I hope you know that. The curse is gone. Bernadette explained that thoroughly. You can choose for yourself now. Even if you," he stopped to swallow, "choose to marry him. There would be no more relapses. It's up to you. And don't make this about what you think might possibly although most likely won't help his kingdom. What do *you* want?"

I looked at him as though he had suddenly grown horns. *What did I want?* How could he not know? I shook my head and rolled my eyes at the stupidity of that question.

"You are the daftest man," I said gently before kissing him thoroughly.

"If I'm reading this correctly, we are still engaged?" he asked once he had caught his breath.

"We are still engaged," I grinned.

I realized Eleanor and Breonna were both trying very hard to be inconspicuous over in the corner all the while smiling from ear to ear. Breonna actually had tears in her eyes. But before I could say anything, the door flew open and Damien sauntered in.

CHAPTER TWENTY-SIX

*A*h, Aurora," Damien addressed me warmly. "I trust you slept well?"

I stared at him. I was starting to wonder if he was more than a little delusional.

"*Claire* is fine," James's voice rumbled angrily.

Damien ignored him completely and held out his hand to me. "Come, darling. I must speak with you alone."

I shook my head in disbelief. "I'm not going anywhere with you."

His smile faltered a little. His eyes darted around in confusion before they hardened and he held out his hand again.

"My dear, it wasn't really a request."

I felt a chill go down my spine as I saw four guards enter behind Damien. I had seen James best more men than this, but what was it Damien had said? It made it harder for him if I was there. My presence gave the enemy leverage. And in this room were three people he loved. I could see him weighing all of this as he clenched and unclenched his fists at his sides. He took one step forward just as Damien instructed one of his guards to take hold of Eleanor and another, Breonna.

"Thomas," Damien addressed the third guard. "Please restrain this man before he makes a foolish decision."

James growled as the guard secured his hands behind his back and around the back of a chair. He then tied his feet. "Careful, James," Damien admonished. "There are dozens more where these guards came from. You know, James, you think too much. You try too hard. You always have. You need to let things go. Like before when we were friends."

"Damien, I will say this once more. We have *never* been friends," James bit out.

Damien shook his head sadly and turned to lead me out of the room. I heard James struggle and I caught his eyes, wild and frightened. He was never frightened. I gulped and took a deep breath, determined to be strong for him. "It will be alright," I mouthed to him. "I love you." I followed Damien and he shut the door behind us.

Damien led me to the library. It was enormous and sumptuously decorated, like everywhere else in this palace. He sat me down on a chaise and started pacing before me.

"Now that you have seen my kingdom, have to reconsidered our original agreement?"

I started to shake my head and he quickly took a seat beside me and grabbed my hands in his own.

"Aurora—Claire, we were happy together in the beginning. Remember? It could be that way again. I really believed what I told you in that village. With your grace and kindness we can be great rulers."

"I can't, Damien. You must see that. There must be other options," I pleaded.

"There aren't any," Damien nearly yelled as he rose from the chaise. "And you may not have a choice, Aurora. You don't know. You don't know everything."

"What are you talking about, Damien?"

The crazed look in his eyes was starting to scare me. It was a look of wild desperation. He shoved his face close to me until his nose was just inches from mine

"Would you like to know how I came to hear of you and your story?" Damien asked.

"You—you heard the legend from a traveling minstrel." I hated the tremble in my voice.

He smirked. "That's the story I came up with, but in reality I found a record here in this library. It was a collection of correspondence between the dark fairy queen Zora and my great-grandfather. You see, of all his many women, she seemed to be quite a favorite of his. He treated her with the respect and adoration she deserved and she rewarded him by protecting his kingdom with her magic and influence. It was her help that caused him to be able to take over your abandoned lands. When she became pregnant with his child she left the boy to be raised as a legitimate royal heir since my great-grandfather's own wife was barren. In her last epistle she explained that in one hundred years time, if a man kissed the sleeping princess within the great thorn walls he could marry her and solidify the control over both kingdoms. Once this future man obtained his treasured daughter, her revenge on your father would be complete. Her son, my grandfather, died relatively young from a weak constitution and my idiot of a father knew nothing of this. Obviously, the records had been left in the library for someone worthy of the knowledge. And clearly that was me. With my people on the brink of revolution, I needed money. And I needed a reason to unite the people. I forced James to help me find you. Poor James. I should have known he would do something so stupid as to fall in love you. Ever since I had him knighted, I've had a feeling he meant to continue to try and rise above his station." He shook his head as though pityingly remorseful.

"Damien," I began. "Do you honestly think that I would marry you now? After knowing you've ruined countless women, kidnapped and held two women hostage in order to blackmail your strongest knight, conspired to keep control of my kingdom as well as yours, and last but not least, knowing you are a direct descendent of the very woman who's curse caused me more anguish than I can even begin to explain?" My voice escalated along with my body as I rose from the chaise and shouted at him in my anger.

"No, Aurora, no," he tried to soothe me. "That proves that we are meant to be together."

"My name is Claire!" I screamed.

"Your name is Aurora," he said as though I were a small child. "Claire is ordinary. Much like you are turning out to be. Your freckles, your clumsiness, your average voice and talents. You are turning out to be not at all as I expected, but I am willing to look past that. Perhaps we can arrange with the fairy council to return some of your gifts."

With each word he said I felt a small stab in my heart. I fought it. I thought of James. He loved me for who I was. I didn't need those gifts. I was enough without them. But then all I could see was myself tripping, my dirty face and freckles, my tongue-tied stupors in the face of nervousness. Was he right? Was I lacking now? I had only known this new me for a short time. The perfect Aurora had been with me for years. I started to cry and I swiped at my tears in frustration. Damien took my other hand and patted it gently.

"It will be alright. We will marry and James can go back to being a farmer. He'll be happy there. Our kingdoms will remain united. I will rule and you will support me with your grace and beauty."

Something in me snapped. And I found myself again.

"No." I said clearly, my voice low and dangerous, even to my own ears.

"I beg your pardon?"

"I said, no."

"But you can't—"

I cut him off.

"No, you listen to me for a minute, Damien. I don't think anyone has ever told you *no* before. Is that it? You've always gotten your way. You've always had your messes cleaned up for you. Well, I'm sorry for that. I'm sorry that you were raised that way, but that does not mean that I have to suffer so that you can maintain your twisted illusion of reality. I will not be part of this. We were both of us raised sheltered in different ways. But you can choose to change. I have chosen to stop accepting what happens to me and to fight for my own future, no matter what it is. And so I will not choose this. I will not let you force me."

Damien's mouth had slowly dropped as I continued my speech. Then he shook his head and plastered one of his phony charming smiles on his face and grabbed me. His fingers dug into my arms. I wanted to wipe the awful smirk off his face. I wanted to hit him as hard as I could. As hard as I would never be able to hit Zora.

My instinct was to shrink away so instead I lunged forward, startling Damien so that he released my arms. I took advantage of his momentary unbalance and smashed my fist into his nose. My hand ached with the agony of connecting with solid flesh and bone, but Damien was worse off. He held his nose as it spurted blood and he sank to the ground in shock.

I ran.

Once in the corridor, I saw two guards stationed just outside the library.

"His Highness needs assistance," I yelled, hoping to sound distressed, which I was. They rushed to enter the room and I sprinted down the hall before they could realize their mistake. I tried to remember the direction back toward Eleanor and Breonna's chamber when I suddenly stopped. That would be the first place they would look for me. Not to mention all the guards there to watch James. I didn't know where to go. If I knew James, he had probably been figuring out a way to escape and get to me. He didn't know where I was. I didn't—

A hand reached around my face and smothered the cry coming from my mouth. I fought down the panic that threatened to overwhelm me. I needed to stay conscious. I needed to fight. I turned in his arms, expecting to see Damien, but instead finding a face I had never seen before. He wore a royal guard's uniform and had dark hair and a thin mustache. He had a wicked leer on his face and the cruelest eyes I had ever seen.

"Hello, Princess," he snarled. "We've been so anxious to meet you."

I renewed my struggling with increased fervor. He laughed and stroked a finger down one cheek.

"I can see why Prince Damien is so taken with you." His lecherous smile made me sick.

My tears started again. Feelings of fear mingled with fresh anger. I gritted my teeth and spat in his face. He swore and I didn't have time to react before the back of his hand shot out and hit the side of my face. Everything went dark for just a moment and then I saw blinding light before blinking furiously, trying to clear my head. He pulled out a dagger and pressed it to my side as he led me back toward the library.

He suddenly shifted me so that my back was in front of him while he kept a strong grip under my neck across my shoulders. I gasped as I felt the dagger, only this time he had brought it up so that it pressed in just below my chin.

"Well what do we have here," he snarled.

And then I saw James. How had he escaped? I tried to smile, but I was starting to shake.

"Let her go," James warned through clenched teeth.

"I don't think you're in any position to be making demands," the guard goaded. He pressed the dagger closer and I winced. James held up his hands. I saw the panic in his eyes and I knew that Damien had won.

"James," I tried to call out to him through my tears, but the guard cut me off, roughly jerking me toward him and angling the tip more aggressively into my skin. I felt a warm trickle of blood run down throat and I closed my eyes against the terror erupting within me. Just one drop of blood. That scarlet orb growing bigger until it made its way slowly down my skin.

I saw Zora's face again. It taunted me. I felt the helplessness and fear that had constantly hung over me. And then anger and adrenaline replaced every feeling of weakness. I was finished with waiting for someone to come protect me. To modify spells for me. To rescue me.

I opened my eyes and looked straight at James. And then Damien rushed up beside him followed by more guards. I saw Damien's smug smile. I suddenly felt calm. I saw the fear and apprehension in James's eyes but I also saw his faith in me. I felt him willing me to be strong.

In a blur of motion I threw my head back and it connected sharply with the guard's nose. My head reeled, but I ignored it. I took advantage of his slackened grip and shoved his hand holding the dagger away from me and elbowed him with all my strength in his stomach. The knife fell to the ground and I heard James charging up behind me. I looked the guard in the eyes and brought my knee up sharply into his groin. He cried out in pain and fell backward. I shoved him hard and his head thudded against the wall as he crumpled into an unconscious heap on the ground.

James reached me then and lifted me into his arms. Only then did I realize that our fight was not over. We both turned to face Damien and his guards. Damien looked shocked. So did his companions. Damien reached out to me. I shook my head and pressed closer to James. He brought his feet further apart and stood waiting. We were both ready.

"Come on, then," James almost smiled with a wave of his hand, beckoning. "We all know I've faced worse." He used Damien's own words and Damien's face paled.

The first guard lunged and James brought him down with one punch to the side of the head. The next two he disabled by blows to the ribs and other various organs. He kicked the next in the chin sending him to the ground in a crumple of unconsciousness while spinning to grab his next opponent and throw him into the last guard. They both landed in a heap, cracking their heads against the massive stone walls.

I blinked.

Damien turned and ran.

James quickly turned to me, grabbed my hand, and rushed me through the halls toward who knows where.

"Where are we going?" I gasped.

"Somewhere safe," he answered cryptically. Did such a place exist here?

After what seemed like a hundred more twists and turns and flights of stairs we entered a cellar-like room under a quiet stairway. The moment he shut the door he turned and pulled me into his arms. As I felt them encircle me I exhaled, all of my strength spent. I was shaking. James kissed my face. I wrapped my arms around his neck.

"I've never been so proud in my life," he breathed. "And I've also never been so grateful I let someone practice fighting on me."

I smiled crookedly into the warm skin of the hollow of his neck. It was then that I realized we were not alone. Eleanor and Breonna and someone else I could only assume was a friend of some kind surrounded us, exclaiming their relief at our safety. James quickly told them how I had taken care of myself and I blushed with pleasure at his praise. Of course he left out the fact that he had defeated six men before I could even form a coherent thought.

The man I didn't recognize introduced himself as Timothy. He worked as a trainer for the knights in the palace and had befriended James long ago.

"He is one of the few truly good men that I found in this place," James explained, squeezing Timothy's shoulder and smiling with fondness. Timothy returned the sentiment.

"I hate to dampen the mood, but what is the plan?" I asked. "And how on earth did you escape?"

"Ah, you think so little of me that you imagine a mere binding of my hands and feet would be enough to stop me when your life hangs in the balance?" James teased.

I rolled my eyes at him and waited for his explanation.

"The Duke of Ellsworth has come," Eleanor took up the narrative. "A guard ran to our room to inform the others stationed there of the incoming army and that was all the distraction that James needed."

"The Duke is here?" I clarified, not daring to believe.

"It's true," James confirmed. "Their army along with the People's Army are fighting to get through the gates as we speak. Several palace guards have turned on their own and have joined the other side. Which brings me to another point . . ." His voice trailed off and I got a sinking feeling in my stomach.

"You're not planning to join in, are you?" I demanded, even as I already knew the answer.

"I'll be fine, Claire," he reassured me.

"Then I'm coming with you," I said flatly. When he started to protest, I continued. "You saw what I did before, I can help." It was silly really, comparing that to what he had done the last two days. But I wasn't backing down on this.

"Claire, that is out of the question," he insisted.

"But you said yourself—"

"Yes, you did well. You did marvelously. But these people will have weapons. Actual weapons used for war, and you didn't train for that."

I kept my jaw stubbornly set.

"When I am finished here we'll go home and I'll train you in weaponry. You can even be the first female general for all I care, but please, you have to let me go and promise not to follow me," he begged. He shook his head and rolled his eyes. It reminded me so much of our early days of friendship I almost cried.

James bent to hug his mother and sister quickly and then shook Timothy's hand as he had promised to stay and guard our cellar. He then turned to me and touched my shoulder. I tried to remain aloof. He turned to go, but I threw myself at him before he could leave. He grabbed me and held me so tight, I could barely breath.

"Please don't be too brave," I whispered. He pulled back and grinned. Then he kissed me once and walked through the door.

CHAPTER TWENTY-SEVEN

I paced in the cellar. It was a small space so it could hardly be called proper pacing, but I did my best. I couldn't take this. I quickly thought back over every word exchanged with James before he left. I had let him go, but I had made no promise. I slowly smiled. I beckoned Eleanor over to me. She left her mother's side where she was conversing with Timothy.

"Eleanor," I whispered. "You have to help me get out of here."

Her eyes widened and she started to shake her head.

"Please," I begged. "I cannot stay here and do nothing. I won't tell James it was you. I just can't stay in this place while waiting for things to happen. I promise I won't get too involved, but I have to know what is going on. Please help me. Please create a distraction for Timothy while I slip out the door." I could see Eleanor struggle within her at what to do. Finally I saw her concession in her eyes and my own filled with tears of gratitude. I squeezed her shoulders and beamed at her. She shook her head at me like the crazy person I was and walked toward the back of the cellar. Once there she screamed and stumbled. It was very convincing. I almost ran back to assist. But I caught myself as I heard her exclaim something to Timothy and Breonna about a spider or a mouse. I slipped out the door before I could be sure.

Once outside, I ran. I sprinted back, retracing my steps to the best of my abilities. I heard riots and fighting both within and outside of the palace. I had to get to a higher vantage point. I found a back stairwell and climbed until my legs threatened to collapse. I ended up on a balcony overlooking the main courtyard. I covered my mouth at the carnage I saw. But I could see the royal guards and army retreating. I retreated behind a pillar and sprinted over to another side, looking into a separate courtyard. I found James. Somehow in all the commotion I found him. He was taller and blonder than anyone around him it seemed. I watched, anxious, as he fought beside the duke's men. Having vanquished their immediate threats, the men ran off toward another area of battle. James stopped for a moment, examining a fallen comrade and helping him to the side. Just then I saw a palace guard sneaking up, holding a sword poised to strike James from behind. I screamed James's name and he whirled just in time to side step the blow. He took the sword easily and punched the man as hard as I had ever seen him punch anyone. The guard crumpled to the floor where James bound his hands and feet. All the while glaring up at me on the balcony. Just as James started to run for me, we heard the call for a ceasefire and a great cheer from the People's Army. James and I stared at each other in relief and then I whirled to run down the stairs and join him.

I reached him halfway down the stairs as he was running up. Before I could say anything, he threw me over his shoulder.

"You have got to be the most infuriating princess ever born," he muttered.

"You're welcome for saving your life," I said, trying to maintain a sense of dignity as my stomach bounced on his shoulder. "Ooof, that one hurt. You're doing that on purpose," I groaned. "James, put me down. The battle is won. I'm safe now." He finally obeyed me when we had finished descending the staircase.

"I'm safe now and so are you. Thanks to me," I insisted with a smirk.

James looked as though he couldn't make up his mind if he should kiss me or box my ears. He settled on a bear hug. As he squeezed the breath out of me, he said, "You win, Sass. Thank you for saving my life."

I pulled back and smiled mischievously.

"That's what I'm here for."

EPILOGUE

Once the fighting ended, everything cleared up quite quickly. Damien was found cowering in a safe room with his father and some of their advisors. They conceded victory to the duke and were sentenced to exile on an island in the Eastern Sea. The duke was not perfect by any means, but he started immediately on reforms after his coronation and the people settled happily into a new way of life. Due to James's help in the battle and after some deliberations between myself and the duke, we decided to again divide the kingdoms and live as allies. Because of the precarious nature of the whole kingdom, no one had much of a problem with the new boundaries. They simply wanted change.

Once things were settled, James brought me and his family back to Kalynbrae. I felt bad about taking them away from their home, but Breonna assured me there had been few happy memories there since her husband's passing. I promised Eleanor plenty of space to roam out of doors.

A messenger had been dispatched to Kalynbrae as soon as the battle was won to alert my father to the news and to tell him we would be following soon. James made sure to include in the message that they should prepare for a wedding.

And what a wedding it was. Fitting for the kind of absolutely wonderful marriage it turned out to be. James became a prince, albeit a somewhat chagrined and uncomfortable looking one. During the banquet after his coronation he whispered a promise to me that he would try to grow used to the ornate crown that sat atop his handsome head. I in turn promised that he didn't have to wear it *all* the time.

One of my maids tried to cover up my freckles while preparing me for the wedding celebration. I stopped her quickly and told her I didn't need any more beauty powder. Now, when I looked at my freckles I saw in each one some new part of my personality. Some imperfections. Some strengths. All of them aspects of who I was. And I was proud of them. However, I don't think I fully came to appreciate freckles until I saw them on the angelic nose of my firstborn son. I suggested we name him William after James's father. My husband agreed with tears in his eyes. William was followed by three more little princes and princesses. Bernadette came as our special guest to every naming ceremony, though the practice of fairy gifts had been officially banned, and she proudly admired each baby as what she considered to be a direct outcome of her handiwork. And in a way, each tiny miracle was result of her influence in my life.

Following my father's death many years later, James and I carried on his legacy of governing with fairness and compassion during our reign. When we weren't attending to our official duties, James enjoyed training with the knights and soldiers, helping the gardeners with their crops, and counting my freckles. I filled my time painting (more of a challenge after my gifts were taken away and therefore, more enjoyable), teaching my children to ride, and having my freckles counted. We played with and loved our children to the point of excess. We relished in telling them stories of evil princes, enchanted forests, and magical kisses.

Most importantly though, we taught them to live and to love.

The End

DISCUSSION QUESTIONS

1. How does losing her gifts affect Claire? How do we base our own worth on our outward attributes or what people think and say about us?

2. James was born to be a farmer. Had his father not died, do you think James would have been happy with that life? Do you think he will be happy being a king?

3. Claire fell in love with James in part because he saw her for who she really is. What made him able to do that? How important is it for you to be seen as you truly are?

4. Damien reveals his true character throughout the story but especially at the end. What made Claire so willing to fall for him in the beginning and what makes her finally start to see him for who he really is by the end?

5. Damien refuses to call Claire anything but Aurora. How and why does this bother Claire and what is the deeper significance of his choice and these two names?

6. Claire describes her parents as good and loving. How do they show that goodness and love? Do you agree with their parenting

choices? If in their places, how might you have handled things differently?

7. Throughout the story, Claire becomes more and more independent and empowered. Why is this important? How is it different from the way she lived before the curse? How important is it for you to take responsibility for you own choices and actions?

8. In what ways do Claire and James complement each other in their relationship? How are they different? What do they have in common?

ACKNOWLEDGMENTS

irst, I'd like to thank my family, especially Brandon, for believing in me and never letting me stop believing in myself. Your special mix of optimism, realism, and determination are exactly what every writer needs in their number one cheerleader. Plus, you're easy on the eyes and never stop making me laugh. I love you more than you know. Hudson, Layna, Beckett, and Maisie. You have each influenced me in a hundred million ways. I love counting your freckles, kissing your scratches, and reading books together for hours when we should be doing math. Thank you for your unconditional love and patience.

My parents, Marlene and Kelly Gallacher. I cannot begin to thank you enough. You have taught and continue to teach me every minute of your existence. Thank you for loving me, for rooting for me, for supporting me, and for giving so much of yourselves to me. And thank you for printing out my first story about kittens when I was five years old and not laughing when I said I wanted to be an author like J. M. Barrie when I grew up. You both took me seriously and believed me. I could tell even then and I love you for it.

To my sisters and brother (Kenna, Cailey, Maddie, Cami, and Brigham), I thank you for your love and support and for making my childhood the most magical one I can imagine. I don't know of many groups as close as we are. What a merry little band of crazies we are. Thank you for reading my book and for swooning in all the right parts. If you ever read something really positive and endearing about a character in my stories and it reminds you of yourself, you are probably right.

Marriage has given me so many more family members to love and cherish. Thank you, Mike and Lorrie Doyle, for raising an amazing son and for loving me like a daughter. To all my brothers- and sisters-in-law, thank you for being my friends and favorites.

Megan Hendershot, Liz Washburn, and Ashleigh Hansen all read early, very rough drafts of this book and loved it anyway. Thank you for that. Your friendships mean the world to me. Becca Hall Johnson saw me through various workshopping drafts during college and never stopped encouraging me and making me feel like what I was doing would be worth it in the end. And Megan Favero and Anna Hargadon Peterson helped me plant the seeds of the story very early on. Thank you for running around our Northern California woods with me, playing fairies and gypsies and orphan girls who broke all the rules to save their communities (girl power!). I have been blessed with great and good friends. Thank you so much.

I have had many inspiring teachers and mentors along the way who have helped shape and influence my writing and confidence in many ways. To list only a few: Diana Tanner, Ron Woods, Lori Haddock, Lisa Hale, Patrick Madden, and Kerry Soper. Thank you for encouraging me, inspiring me, and for being patient with my wordiness.

Thank you to everyone at Cedar Fort who has helped me along the way. Hali Bird and Jessica Romrell: Thank you for your clear, concise, and wonderfully encouraging editing! Thank you for believing in me and my book. Thank you, Priscilla Chaves, for the absolutely beautiful cover design. And thank you, Vikki Downs, for being patient with me and my author self who is apparently very introverted.

Lastly, I'd like to thank my Heavenly Father for His patience, love, and encouragement through good and bad days. And for putting this love of letters and words and stories in my heart in the first place.

ABOUT THE AUTHOR

*B*rittlyn Gallacher Doyle was born and raised in Northern California, where she spent most of her days reading, writing, and playing outside with her four sisters and one brother. While she was a teenager, her family moved to Salzburg, Austria for three years, which she credits as one of the most magical and illuminating periods of her life. She graduated from Brigham Young University in humanities and English after spending four years studying, playing, and studying some more (sometimes abroad—which was her favorite). Brittlyn enjoys music, dancing in her kitchen, avoiding laundry, going on walks, swimming in lakes and oceans, twirling with her children, being outside, and traveling whenever and wherever possible. She currently lives in Pleasant Grove, Utah with her hilarious husband, Brandon, and her four adorably spirited children who are quite patient with her and indulge her in dancing parades around the house when she really should be homeschooling them. Brittlyn grew up reading enormous quantities of fairytale retellings and couldn't be more excited to be joining this grand and glorious tradition.

Scan to Visit

wakingbeautybook.com